THE NEW MOTHER

(and other stories)

Lucy Lane Clifford

Illustrations by
D M Mitchell

This book is a work of fiction. The names, characters and incidents portrayed in it are all drawn from the author's imagination. Any resemblance to real persons living or dead, events or localities is entirely coincidental.

This edition by ONEIROS BOOKS 2012

Copyright this edition
Oneiros Books
in an imprint of Paraphilia Magazine
www.paraphiliamagazine.com

All efforts have been made to contact the person or persons holding the rights to this book.

ISBN 978-1-300-36323-1

CONTENTS

THE BAD GIRL	P1
THE WOODEN DOLL	P4
THE NEW MOTHER	P7
FROM OUTSIDE THE WORLD	P25
THE WHITE RABBITS	P36
THE POOR LITTLE DOLL	P37
THE COBBLER'S CHILDREN	P40
ROUND THE RABBIT HOLES	P46
THE BEAUTIFUL LADY	P54
ROUND THE TEA TABLE	P61
THE BROKEN HORSE	P64
MASTER WILLIE	P65
THE WOODEN HORSE	P73
IN THE MOONLIGHT	P74
TOMMY	P77
THE IMITATION FISH	P80
THE DONKEY ON WHEELS	P85
THE PAPER SHIP	P88
THE THREE LITTLE RAGAMUFFINS	P90
WOODEN TONY	P94
Lucy Lane Clifford (a biographical note)	P134

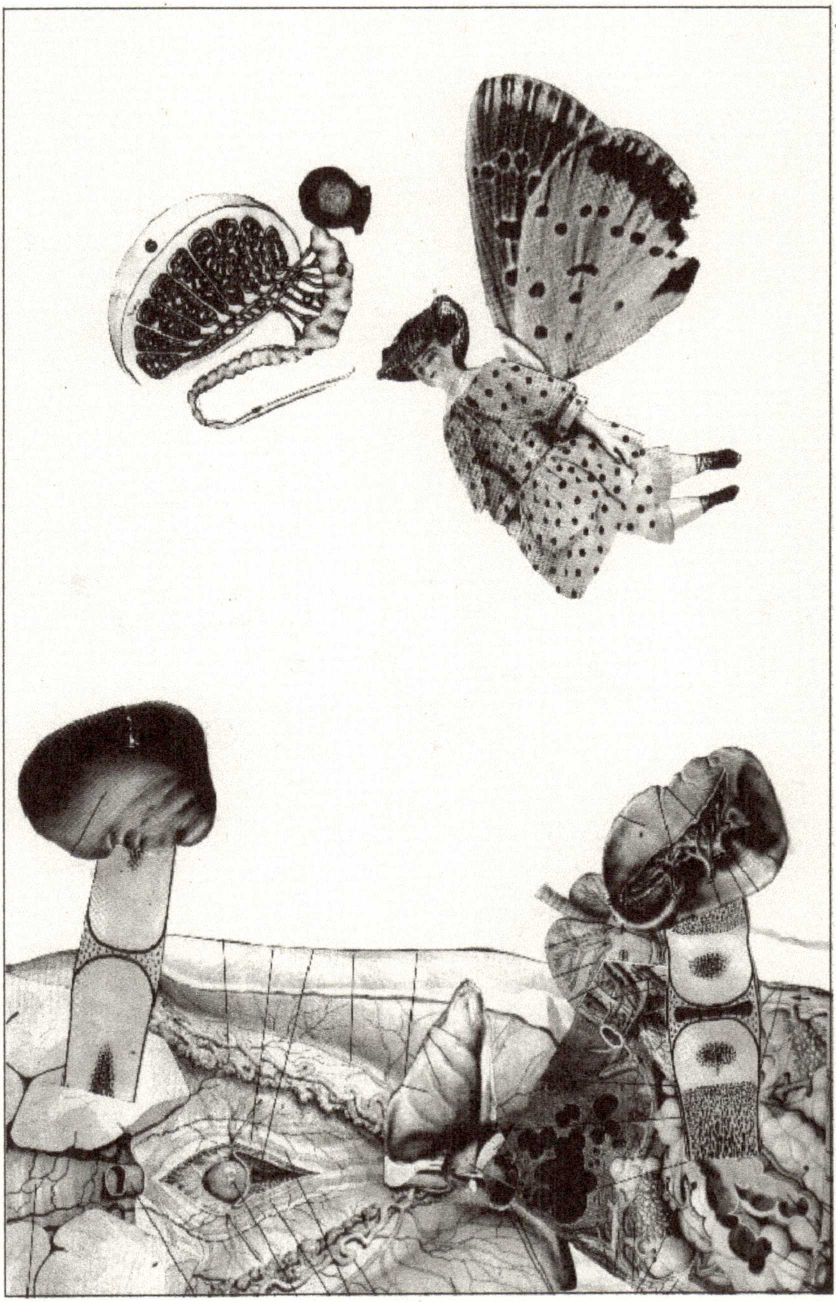

THE BAD GIRL

SHE was always called the bad girl, for she had once, when she was very little, put out her tongue at the postman. She lived alone with her grandmother and her three brothers in the cottage beyond the field, and the girls in the village took no notice of her. The bad girl did not mind this, for she was always thinking of the cuckoo clock. The clock stood in one corner of the cottage, and every hour a door opened at the top of its face, and a little cuckoo came out and called its name just the same number of times that the clock ought to have struck, and called it so loudly and in so much haste that the clock was afraid to strike at all. The bad girl was always wondering whether it was worse for the clock to have a cupboard in its forehead, and a bird that was always hopping in and out, or for the poor cuckoo to spend so much time in a dark little prison.

"If it could only get away to the woods," she said to herself, "who knows but its voice might grow sweet, and even life itself might come to it!"

She thought of the clock so much that her grandmother used to say "Ah, lassie, if you would only think of me sometimes!"

But the bad girl would answer, "You are not in prison, granny dear, and you have not even a bee in your bonnet, let alone a bird in your head. Why should I think of you?"

One day, close by the farm, she saw the big girls from the school gathering flowers.

"Give me one," she said; "perhaps the cuckoo would like it."

But they all cried, "No, no!" and tried to frighten her away. "They are for the little one's birthday. To-morrow she will be seven years old," they said, "and she is to have a crown of flowers and a cake, and all the afternoon we shall play merry games with her."

"Is she unhappy, that you are taking so much trouble for her?" asked the bad girl.

"Oh, no; she is very happy, but it will be her birthday, and we want to make her happier."

"Why?"

"Because we love her," said one;

"Because she is so little," said another;

"Because she is alive," said a third.

"Are all things that live to be loved and cared for?" the bad girl asked, but they were too busy to listen, so she went on her way thinking; and it seemed as if all things round the birds, and bees, and the rustling leaves, and the little tender wild flowers, half hidden in the grass answered, as she went along, "Yes, they are all to be cared for and made happier, if it be possible."

"The cuckoo clock is not alive," she thought.

"Oh, no; it is not alive," the trees answered; "but many things that do not live have voices, and many others are just sign-posts, pointing the way."

"The way! The way to what, and where?"

"We find out for ourselves; we must all find out for ourselves," the trees sighed and whispered to each other.

As the bad girl entered the cottage, the cuckoo called out its name eleven times, but she did not even look up. She walked straight across to the chair by the fireside, and kneeling down, kissed her granny's hands.

THE WOODEN DOLL

THE wooden doll had no peace. My dears, if ever you are a doll, hope to be a rag doll, or a wax doll, or a doll full of sawdust apt to ooze out, or a china doll easy to break anything in the world rather than a good strong wooden doll with a painted head and movable joints, for that is indeed a sad thing to be. Many a time the poor wooden doll wished it were a tin train, or a box of soldiers, or a woolly lamb, or anything on earth rather than what it was. It never had any peace; it was taken up and put down at all manners of odd moments, made to go to bed when the children went to bed, to get up when they got up, be bathed when they were bathed, dressed when they were dressed, taken out in all weathers, stuffed into their satchels when they went to school, left about in corners, dropped on stairs, forgotten, neglected, bumped, banged, broken, glued together, anything and everything it suffered, until many a time it said sadly enough to its poor little self, "I might as well be a human being at once and be done with it!"

And then it fell to thinking about human beings; what strange creatures they were, always going about, though none carried them save when they were very little; always sleeping and waking, and eating and drinking, and laughing and crying, and talking and walking, and doing this and that and the other, never resting for long together, or seeming as if they could be still for even a single day.

"They are always making a noise," thought the wooden doll; "they are always talking and walking about, always moving things and doing things, building up and pulling down, and making and unmaking for ever and for ever, and never are they quiet. It is lucky that we are not all human beings, or the world would be worn out in no time, and there would not be a corner left in which to rest a poor doll's head."

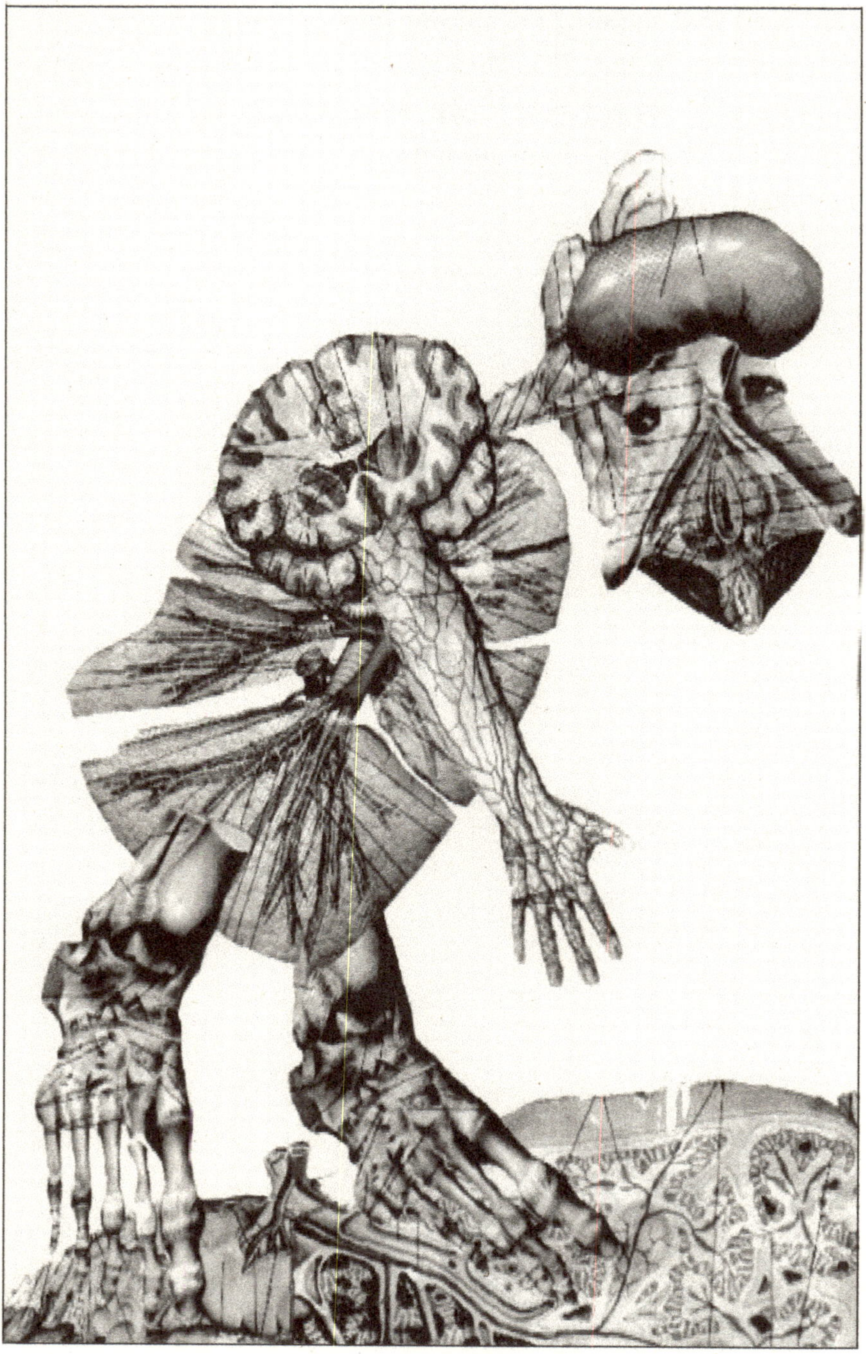

THE NEW MOTHER

I.

The children were always called Blue-Eyes and the Turkey. The elder one was like her dear father who was far away at sea; for the father had the bluest of blue eyes, and so gradually his little girl came to be called after them. The younger one had once, while she was still almost a baby, cried bitterly because a turkey that lived near the cottage suddenly vanished in the middle of the winter; and to console her she had been called by its name.

Now the mother and Blue Eyes and the Turkey and the baby all lived in a lonely cottage on the edge of the forest. It was a long way to the village, nearly a mile and a half, and the mother had to work hard and had not time to go often herself to see if there was a letter at the post-office from the dear father, and so very often in the afternoon she used to send the two children. They were very proud of being able to go alone. When they came back tired with the long walk, there would be the mother waiting and watching for them, and the tea would be ready and the baby crowing with delight; and if by any chance there was a letter from the sea, then they were happy indeed. The cottage room was so cosy; the walls were as white as snow inside as well as out. The baby's high chair stood in one corner, and in another there was a cupboard, in which the mother kept all manner of surprises.

"Dear children," the mother said one afternoon late in the autumn, "it is very chilly for you to go to the village, but you must walk quickly, and who knows but what you may bring back a letter saying that dear father is already on his way to England. Don't be long," the mother said, as she always did before they started. "Go the nearest way and don't look at any strangers you meet, and be sure you do not talk with them."

"No mother," they answered; and then she kissed them and called them dear good children, and they joyfully started on their way.

The village was gayer than usual, for there had been a fair the day before. "Oh, I do wish we had been here yesterday," Blue-Eyes said as they went on to the grocer's which was also the post-office. The post-mistress was very busy and just said, "No letter for you to-day." Then Blue-Eyes and the Turkey turned away to go home. They had left the village and walked some way, and then they noticed, resting against a pile of stones by the wayside, a strange wild-looking girl, who seemed very unhappy. So they thought they would ask her if they could do anything to help her, for they were kind children and sorry indeed for any one in distress.

The girl seemed to be about fifteen years old. She was dressed in very ragged clothes. Round her shoulders there was an old brown shawl. She wore no bonnet. Her hair was coal-black and hung down uncombed and unfastened. She had something hidden under her shawl; on seeing them coming towards her, she carefully put it under her and say upon it. She sat watching the children approach, and did not move or stir till they were within a yard of her; then she wiped her eyes just as if she had been crying bitterly, and looked up.

The children stood still in front of her for a moment, staring at her. "Are you crying?" they asked shyly.

"Perhaps you have lost yourself?" they said gently.

But the girl answered promptly, "Certainly not. Why, you have just found me. Besides, she added, "I live in the village."

The children were surprised at this, for they had never seen her before, and yet they thought they knew all the village folk by sight.

Then the Turkey, who had an inquiring mind, put a question. "What are you sitting on?" she asked.

"On a peardrum," the girl answered.

"What is a peardrum?" they asked.

"I am surprised at your not knowing," the girl answered. "Most people in good society have one." And then she pulled it out and showed it to them. It was a curious instrument, a good deal like a guitar in shape; it had three strings, but only two pegs by which to tune them. But the strange thing about the peardrum was not the music it made, but a little square box attached to one side.

"Where did you get it?" the children asked.

"I bought it," the girl answered.

"Didn't it cost a great deal of money?" they asked.

"Yes," answered the girl, slowly, nodding her head, "it cost a great deal of money. I am very rich," she added.

"You don't look rich," they said, in as polite a voice as possible.

"Perhaps not," the girl answered cheerfully.

At this, the children gathered courage, and ventured to remark, "You look rather shabby."

"Indeed?" said the girl in a voice of one who had heard a pleasant but surprising statement. "A little shabbiness is very respectable." she added in a satisfied voice. "I must really tell them this," she continued. And the children wondered what she meant. She opened the little box by the side of the peardrum, and said, just as if she were speaking to someone who could hear her, "They say I look rather shabby; it is quite lucky isn't it?"

"Why, you are not speaking to any one!" they said, more surprised than ever.

"Oh dear, yes! I am speaking to them both."

"Both?" they said, wondering.

"Yes. I have here a little man dressed as a peasant, and little woman to match. I put them on the lid of the box and when I play they dance most beautifully."

"Oh! let us see; do let us see!" the children cried.

Then the village girl looked at them doubtfully. "Let you see!" she said slowly. "Well, I am not sure that I can. Tell me, are you good?"

"Yes, yes," they answered eagerly, "we are very good!"

"Then it's quite impossible," she answered, and resolutely closed the lid of the box.

They stared at her in astonishment. "But we are good," they cried, thinking she must have misunderstood them. "We are very good. Then can't you let us see the little man and woman?"

"Oh dear, no!" the girl answered. "I only show them to naughty children. And the worse the children the better do the man and woman dance."

She put the peardrum carefully under her ragged cloak, and prepared to go on her way. "I really could not have believed that you were good," she said reproachfully, as if they accused themselves of some great crime. "Well good day."

"Oh, but we will be naughty," they said in despair.

"I am afraid you couldn't," she answered, shaking her head. "It requires a great deal of skill to be naughty well."

And swiftly she walked away, while the children felt their eyes fill with tears, and their hearts ache with disappointment.

"If we had only been naughty," they said, "we should have seen them dance."

"Suppose," said the Turkey, "we try to be naughty today; perhaps she would let us see them tomorrow."

"But, oh!" said Blue-Eyes, "I don't know how to be naughty; no one ever taught me."

The Turkey thought for a few minutes in silence. "I think I can be naughty if I try," she said. "I'll try to-night."

"Oh, don't be naughty without me!" she cried. "It would be so unkind of you. You know I want to see the little man and woman just as much as you do. You are very, very unkind."

And so, quarreling and crying, they reached their home.

Now, when their mother saw them, she was greatly astonished, and, fearing they were hurt, ran to meet them.

"Oh, my children, oh, my dear, dear children," she said; "what is the matter?"

But they did not dare tell their mother about the village girl and the little man and woman, so they answered, "Nothing is the matter," and cried all the more.

"Poor children!" the mother said to herself, "They are tired, and perhaps they are hungry; after tea they will be better." And she went back to the cottage, and made the fire blaze; and she put the kettle on to boil, and set the tea-things on the table. Then she went to the little cupboard and took out some bread and cut it on the table, and said in a loving voice, "Dear little children, come and have your tea. And see, there is the baby waking from her sleep; she will crow at us while we eat."

But the children made no answer to the dear mother; they only stood still by the window and said nothing.

"Come, children," the mother said again. "Come, Blue-Eyes, and come, my Turkey; here is nice sweet bread for tea." Then suddenly she looked up and saw that the Turkey's eyes were full of tears.

"Turkey!" she exclaimed, "my dear little Turkey! What is the matter? Come to mother, my sweet." And putting the baby down, she held out her arms, and the Turkey ran swiftly into them.

"Oh, mother," she sobbed, "oh, dear mother! I do so want to be naughty. I do so want to be very, very naughty."

And then Blue-Eyes left her chair also, and rubbing her face against her mother's shoulder, cried sadly. "And so do I mother. Oh, I'd give anything to be very, very naughty."

"But, my dear children," said the mother, in astonishment, "Why do you want to be naughty?"

"Because we do; oh, what shall we so?" they cried together.

"I should be very angry if you were naughty. But you could not be, for you love me," the mother answered.

"Why couldn't we?" they asked.

Then the mother thought a while before she answered; and she seemed to be speaking rather to herself than to them.

"Because if one loves well," she said gently, "one's love is stronger than all bad feelings in one, and conquers them."

"We don't know what you mean," they cried; "and we do love you; but we want to be naughty."

"Then I should know you did not love me," the mother said.

"If we were very, very, very naughty, and wouldn't be good, what then?"

"Then," said the mother sadly--and while she spoke her eyes filled with tears, and a sob almost choked her — "then," she said, "I should have to go away and leave you, and to send home a new mother, with glass eyes and a wooden tail."

II.

"Good-day," said the village girl, when she saw Blue-Eyes and the Turkey approach. She was again sitting by the heap of stones, and under her shawl the peardrum was hidden.

"Are the little man and woman there?" the children asked.

"Yes, thank you for inquiring after them," the girl answered; "they are both here and quite well. The little woman has heard a secret--she tells it while she dances."

"Oh do let us see," they entreated.

"Quite impossible, I assure you," the girl answered promptly. "You see you are good."

"Oh!" said Blue-Eyes, sadly; "but mother says if we are naughty she will go away and send home a new mother, with glass eyes and a wooden tail."

"Indeed," said the girl, still speaking in the same unconcerned voice, "that is what they all say. They all threaten that kind of thing. Of course really there are no mothers with glass eyes and wooden tails; they would be much too expensive to make." And the common sense of this remark the children saw at once.

"We think you might let us see the little man and woman dance."

"The kind of thing you would think," remarked the village girl.

"But will you if we are naughty?" they asked in despair.

"I fear you could not be naughty--that is, really--even if you tried," she said scornfully.

"But if we are very naughty tonight, will you let us see them tomorrow?"

"Questions asked to-day are always best answered to-morrow," the girl said blithely; "I must really go and play a little to myself."

For a few minutes the children stood looking after her, then they broke down and cried. The Turkey was the first to wipe away her tears. "Let us go home and be very naughty," she said; "then perhaps she will let us see them tomorrow."

And that afternoon the dear mother was solely distressed, for, instead of sitting at their tea as usual with smiling happy faces, they broke their mugs and threw their bread and butter on the floor, and when the mother told them to do one thing they carefully did another, and only stamped their feet with rage when she told them to go upstairs until they were good.

"Do you remember what I told you I should do if you were very, very naughty?" she asked sadly.

"Yes, we know, but it isn't true," they cried. "There is no mother with a wooden tail and glass eyes, and if there were we should just stick pins into her and send her away; but there is none."

Then the mother became really angry, and sent them off to bed, but instead of crying and being sorry at her anger, they laughed for joy, and sat up and sang merry songs at the top of their voices.

The next morning quite early, without asking leave from the mother, the children got up and ran off as fast as they could to look for the village girl. She was sitting as usual by the heap of stones with the peardrum under her shawl.

"Now please show us the little man and woman," they cried, "and let us hear the peardrum. We were very naughty last night." But the girl kept the peardrum carefully hidden.

"So you say," she answered. "You were not half naughty enough. As I remarked before, it requires a great deal of skill to be naughty well."

"But we broke our mugs, we threw our bread and butter on the floor, we did everything we could to be tiresome."

"Mere trifles," answered the village girl scornfully. "Did you throw cold water on the fire, did you break the clock, did you pull all the tins down from the walls, and throw them on the floor?"

"No," exclaimed the children aghast, "we did not do that."

"I thought not," the girl answered. "So many people mistake a little noise and foolishness for real naughtiness." And before they could say another word she had vanished.

"We'll be much worse," the children cried, in despair. "We'll go and do all the things she says"; and then they went home and did all these things. And when the mother saw all that they had done she did not scold them as she had the day before, but she just broke down and cried, and said sadly--

"Unless you are good to-morrow, my poor Blue-Eyes and Turkey, I shall indeed have to go away and come back no more, and the new mother I told you of will come to you."

They did not believe her; yet their hearts ached when they saw how unhappy she looked, and they thought within themselves that when they once had seen the little men and woman dance, they would be good to the dear mother for ever afterwards.

The next morning, before the birds were stirring, the children crept out of the cottage and ran across the fields. They found the village girl sitting by the heap of stones, just as if it were her natural home.

"We have been very naughty," they cried. "We have done all the things you told us; now will you show us the little man and woman?" The girl looked at them curiously. "You really seem quite excited," she said in her usual voice. "You should be calm."

"We have done all the things you told us," the children cried again, "and we do so long to hear the secret. We have been so very naughty, and mother says she will go away today and send home a new mother if we are not good."

"Indeed," said the girl. "Well, let me see. When did your mother say she would go?"

"But if she goes, what shall we do?" they cried in despair. "We don't want her to go; we love her very much."

"You had better go back and be good, you are really not clever enough to be anything else; and the little woman's secret is very important; she never tells it for make-believe naughtiness."

"But we did all the things you told us," the children cried.

"You didn't throw the looking-glass out of the window, or stand the baby on its head."

"No, we didn't do that," he children gasped.

"I thought not," the girl said triumphantly. "Well, good-day. I shall not be here to-morrow."

"Oh, but don't go away," they cried. "Do let us see them just once."

"Well, I shall go past your cottage at eleven o'clock this morning," the girl said. "Perhaps I shall play the peardrum as I go by."

"And will you show us the man and woman?" they asked.

"Quite impossible, unless you have really deserved it; make-believe naughtiness is only spoilt goodness. Now if you break the looking-glass and do the things that are desired..."

"Oh, we will," they cried. "We will be very naughty till we hear you coming."

Then again the children went home, and were naughty, oh, so very, very naughty that the dear mother's heart ached and her eyes filled with tears, and at last she went upstairs and slowly put on her best gown and her new sun-bonnet, and she dressed the baby all in its Sunday clothes, and then she came down and stood before Blue-Eyes and the Turkey, and just as she did the Turkey threw the looking-glass out the window, and it fell with a loud crash upon the ground.

"Good-bye, my children," the mother said sadly, kissing them. "The new mother will be home presently. Oh, my poor children!" and then weeping bitterly, the mother took the baby in her arms and turned to leave the house.

"But mother, we will be good at half-past eleven, come back at half-past eleven," they cried, "and we'll both be good; we must be naughty till eleven o'clock." But the mother only picked up the little bundle in which she had tied up her cotton apron, and went slowly out at the door. Just be the corner of the fields she stopped and turned, and waved her handkerchief, all wet with tears, to the children at the window; she made the baby kiss its hand; and in a moment mother and baby had vanished from their sight.

Then the children felt their hearts ache with sorrow, and they cried bitterly, and yet they could not believe that she had gone. And the broken clock struck eleven, and suddenly there was a sound, a quick, clanging, jangling sound, with a strange discordant note at intervals. They rushed to the open window, and there they saw the village girl dancing along and playing as she did so.

"We have done all you told us," the children called. "Come and see; and now show us the little man and woman."

The girl did not cease her playing or her dancing, but she called out in a voice that was half speaking half singing. "You did it all badly. You threw the water on the wrong side of the fire, the tin things were not quite in the middle of the room, the clock was not broken enough, and you did not stand the baby on its head."

She was already passing the cottage. She did not stop singing, and all she said sounded like part of a terrible song. "I am going to my own land," the girl sang, "to the land where I was born."

"But our mother is gone," the children cried; "our dear mother will she ever come back?"

"No," sang the girl, "she'll never come back. She took a boat upon the river; she is sailing to the sea; she will meet your father once again, and they will go sailing on."

Then the girl, her voice getting fainter and fainter in the distance, called out once more to them. "Your new mother is coming. She is already on her way; but she only walks slowly, for her tail is rather long, and her spectacles are left behind; but she is coming, she is coming--coming--coming."

The last word died away; it was the last one they ever heard the village girl utter. On she went, dancing on.

Then the children turned, and looked at each other and at the little cottage home, that only a week before had been so bright and happy, so cosy and spotless. The fire was out, the clock all broken and spoilt. And there was the baby's high chair, with no baby to sit in it; there was the cupboard on the wall, and never a sweet loaf on its shelf; and there were the broken mugs, and the bits of bread tossed about, and the greasy boards which the mother had knelt down to scrub until were as white as snow. In the midst of all stood the children, looking at the wreck they had made, their eyes blinded with tears, and their poor little hands clasped in misery.

"I don't know what we shall do if the new mother comes," cried Blue-Eyes. "I shall never, never like any other mother."

The Turkey stopped crying for a minute, to think what should be done. "We will bolt the door and shut the window; and we won't take any notice when she knocks."

All through the afternoon they sat watching and listening for fear of the new mother, but they saw and heard nothing for fear of the new mother, but they saw and heard nothing of her, and gradually they became less and less afraid lest she could come. They fetched a pail of water and washed the floor; they found some rag, and rubbed the tins, they picked up the broken mugs and made the room as neat as they could. There was no sweet loaf to put on the table, but perhaps the mother would bring something from the village, they thought. At last all was ready, and Blue-Eyes and the Turkey washed their faces and their hands, and then sat and waited, for of course they did not believe what the village girl had said about their mother sailing away.

Suddenly, while they were sitting by the fire, they heard a sound as of something heavy being dragged along the ground outside, and then there was a loud and terrible knocking at the door. The children felt their hearts stand still. They knew it could not be their own mother, for she would have turned the handle and tried to come in without any knocking at all.

Again there came a loud and terrible knocking.

"She'll break the door down if she knocks so hard," cried Blue-Eyes.

"Go and put your back to it," whispered the Turkey, "and I'll peep out of the window and try to see if it is really the new mother."

So in fear and trembling Blue-Eyes put her back against the door, and the Turkey went to the window. She could just see a black satin poke bonnet with a frill round the edge, and a long bony arm carrying a black leather bag. From beneath the bonnet there flashed a strange bright light, and Turkey's heart sank and her cheeks turned pale, for she knew it was the flashing of two glass eyes. She crept up to Blue-Eyes. "It is--it is--it is!" she whispered, her voice shaking with fear, "it is the new mother!"

Together they stood with the two little backs against the door. There was a long pause. They thought perhaps the new mother had made up her mind that there was no one at home to let her in, and would go away, but presently the two children heard through the thin wooden door the new mother moved a little, and then say to herself—"I must break the door open with my tail."

For one terrible moment all was still, but in it the children could almost hear her lift up her tail, and then, with a fearful blow, the little painted door cracked and splintered. With a shriek the children darted from the spot and fled through the cottage, and out at the back door into the forest beyond. All night long they stayed in the darkness and the cold, and all the next day and the next, and all through the cold, dreary days and the long dark nights that followed.

They are there still, my children. All through the long weeks and months they have been there, with only green rushes for their pillows and only the brown dead leaves to cover them, feeding on the wild strawberries in the summer, or on the nuts when they hang green; on the blackberries when they are no longer sour in the autumn, and in the winter on the little red berries that ripen in the snow. They wander about among the tall dark firs or beneath the great trees beyond. Sometimes they stay to rest beside the little pool near the copse, and they long and long, with a longing that is greater than words can say, to see their own dear mother again, just once again, to tell her that they'll be good for evermore--just once again.

And still the new mother stays in the little cottage, but the windows are closed and the doors are shut, and no one knows what the inside look like. Now and then, when the darkness has fallen and the night is still, hard in hand Blue-Eyes and the Turkey creep up near the home in which they once were so happy, and with beating hearts they watch and listen; sometimes a blinding flash comes through the window, and they know it is the light from the new mother's glass eyes, or they hear a strange muffled noise, and they know it is the sound of her wooden tail as she drags it along the floor.

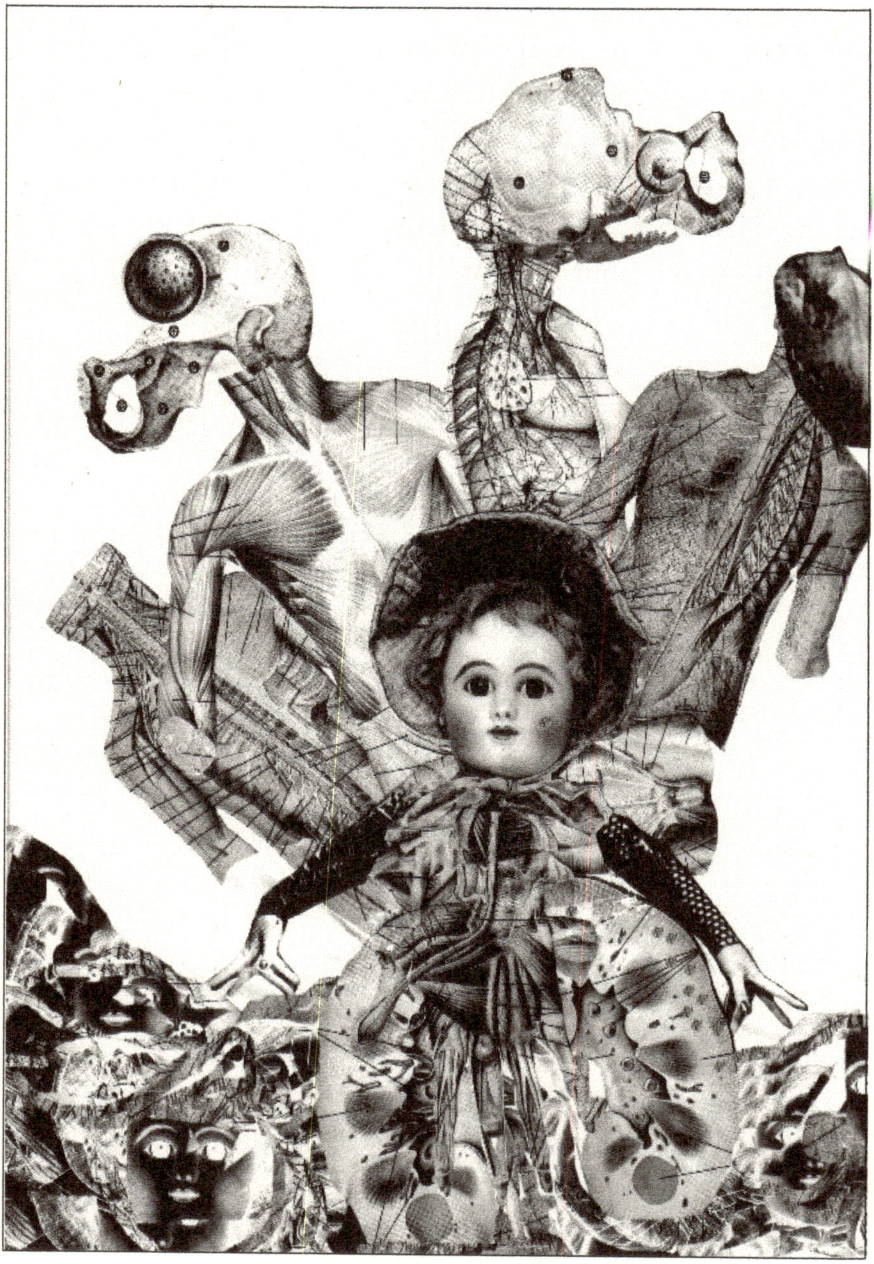

FROM OUTSIDE THE WORLD

SHE wandered about in the sunshine all the day long, over the fields and in the woods, picking the flowers and listening to the birds, and singing strange songs to the river. Suddenly she sat down on a big stone and looked up at the mountain that was just a little too tall for the world, and had to hide its head in the clouds.

"I should like to climb that mountain," she thought; "I want to know what there is on the other side." And the more she thought about it the more did she long to climb. At last she jumped up and washed her feet in a little stream of clear water, and set off as fast as she could for the top of the mountain. It was a long way up, but she sang all the time, and amused herself by wondering if any had ever been lost on the great hills around her,—the hills that stretched away and away as far as she could see,—and if so whether there had been wives and children watching for them at home, watching, and waiting, and weeping, and listening for a footstep that would never come over the heather again, for the sound of a voice that never would speak to them more. "If I could only feel," she sighed, "if I could only understand; oh, I would give the world to know what it is like."

She went slowly down the other side of the mountain. At its foot there was a little town; it was just a very little town, with one street running down the middle of it, and a town-hall in the market-place, and a clock on the town-hall that had lost its long hand, so it pointed to the hours with its short one, and never troubled itself about the minutes.

There were not many people in the town, but they all knew one another and talked about one another, and nobody ever minded his own business, but always some other body's. She stood at one end of the street and looked at the schoolhouse and the toll-bar in the distance, and she walked to the other end and looked at the meadows, and at an old barn, and at the farm-house, which was the last dwelling-place she could see. "It is just the same here as everywhere else, I suppose," she said to herself. "The people laugh and cry, and love and hate, and play that queer game of theirs which consists in one person gaining as much money as he can, and the rest getting as much of it away from him as they can, and the end of it is always the same; the man dies and is forgotten, and the next man goes on. I wonder what it all means." She sat down by the wayside and rested; she watched the people in the street, but no one noticed her. She saw two men pass by; she heard one say to the other —

"It is a fair price; that field is not worth more;" and she said to herself —

"It is the old story, they are talking of money."

A man and woman passed, the woman saying as she did so —

"I am not going to do it for less, I can tell her;" and again the girl said to herself —

"The old story, it is money for ever, money, money, for ever!" She got up and walked a little way, wondering if there were any children in the town, the children would be interesting, she thought. The old people were the world of yesterday; and the grown people were the world of to-day; but the children would be the world of to-morrow: of to-morrow that for ever was on its way, for ever held a promise. There was life in the very word, since only dead men ceased to think of it and to plan for it.

"There is some clue to life I have missed, there is something that I am longing for but cannot grasp. I am for ever feeling as if I ought to be paying myself in as a tribute to some great whole which I cannot see because of the darkness before me," she thought.

"Who are you, girl?" a voice asked suddenly. She looked up and saw a farmer behind her.

"I have come from a cottage over the mountain," the girl answered.

"What have you come for?"

"Just to see and to think," she answered.

"It is waste of time," he said gruffly, and turned away. "Will you have a cup of milk?" he asked suddenly, "for maybe you are tired; go to the house yonder, and say I sent you," and he pointed to the farm-house. She was hungry and thirsty, and glad to do as she was told.

"Why do you offer me milk?" she asked; "I am a stranger."

"Strangers feel thirsty as well as friends," he answered.

The girl went to the farm-house, and when the good wife saw her she made her sit down, and fetched some fresh milk and home-made bread, and bade her rest well before she went on her way.

"I never gave any one a cup of milk or welcome into my cottage in my whole life," the girl thought. "There is some meaning in the world I have not found yet, but it seems a little nearer as I sit and watch the farmer's wife." Then she rose, and, coldly thanking her, went on.

"I will go through the town now," she said to herself. A boy was sitting on the gate at the end of the field. He was gaily dressed: from his cap there hung a gold tassel, and on his finger he wore a ring. The girl stopped and looked at him.

"Where do you live?" she asked.

"I live at the great house up there," he answered, nodding in the direction of the hill. "You can see the flag waving from the tower."

"You must be rich," she said, "for your house is very grand. How did you get all your money?"

"My ancestors won it hundreds of years ago," he answered proudly. "There were great men."

"And are you great?" she asked.

"I am great, for I am rich," he answered.

"And so you have time to think," she said eagerly. "Tell me, do you know all things?"

"No," he said, "I never trouble about them; I am content to live and enjoy my riches."

"I cannot understand it," she sighed; "men are content to work for those they will never see, and to heap up money perchance for fools to spend. Money doesn't make you great," she said scornfully to the boy; "any booby can inherit."

She went down the street, she looked at the faces of the people; on all of them there seemed to be written some history of past days, some record of joy and sorrow, but most of sorrow. "I am very thankful," she thought, "that I shall never know the things they know. I remember once overhearing some poet or dreamer say that in every heart there was a death chamber; there is none is mine; I have no heart to hold one." The townspeople were looking out at their doors, laughing and making merry when any two met; she wondered what it was all about, till suddenly she saw a bridal party go by. "I see now," she said to herself; "these are two people going to marry, and they are rejoicing because they will be together henceforth. One will know when the other sorrows, and one will sit and watch at last by the other's dead face. Why do they rejoice? Oh! I shall never understand it all." She turned out of the street, and went towards the fields again. A boy was loitering on his way from school, and farther on, there sat a man by an easel, on which stood an untouched canvas. The boy looked at the girl.

"What do you learn at school?" she asked.

"All kinds of things," he answered. "I am very happy while I am learning," he added. "And after the lessons come the games."

"What shall you do when you are a man?" she asked.

"I shall go on with the making of the world," he said, and began to sing.

"Why do you want to do that? We all die soon."

"It was made for us, it is ours now, we have to make it for those to come. Even to think of it makes one long to begin."

"But we shall not be here."

"Others will," he laughed, and went on his way still singing.

"Perhaps the artist will tell me something," she thought, and went up to him.

"Have you painted many pictures?" she asked.

"No," he answered, "I have painted none that are worth remembering yet, but I shall some day."

"How do you know?" she asked curiously.

"Because I love the world so much," he answered; "it is very beautiful," he sighed. "I should despair of my own self, but that love makes one so strong; it helps one to do all things."

"Why do you want to paint pictures?" she asked.

"Pictures are messages of light in dark places," he answered. "I want to tell the story of the world's beauty to the cities, so that some of those who live, and work, and have seldom time to rest, and never time to journey, may wander in its fairest places and know them in their hearts." The girl's face became eager as she listened, she felt some dim understanding, and yet why should he care for unknown people in unseen cities?

"And can you do it; can you make pictures that will do this, and where did you get the power?"

"I worked for it; I am working for it still, and some day I shall succeed, as all, who love their work well must."

"Love—what has that to do with it?"

"One must love one's work," he answered. "'For whatever a man loves he can create, and the work of his hands is that in which his soul delighteth.'"

"There is some use in love that makes the world prettier or better," she said; "I understand that, but there is none in love the end of which is parting and sorrow."

"The one is the outcome of the other," he said. "As death is the consequence of life, so is sorrow the outcome of joy, the price we pay for it somehow or at some time."

"But if that is so," the girl said, "surely you should bear your sorrows in silence, and not cry out as if your happiness had been over-dear."

"Ah," said the painter, taking up his brush, "that is an easy thing to say, and a sorry one to hear," and then he began to work, and the girl went towards the hill.

"I will go home," she said to herself; "I am no wiser than when I came." She passed a cottage at the foot of the hill; an old woman sat by the door knitting. Suddenly the girl stopped.

"May I come in and rest a bit, mother?" she asked.

"Yes, my child," the woman answered; and she took the girl into the cottage and made her sit down by the fire, and gave her food and drink, and watched her while she rested. Suddenly the girl looked up.

"Mother," she said, "I have been wandering through the little town looking at the people, only at the outside of their lives, and hearing just their most careless words. Tell me, what does it all mean? Why do they go on eager for life which is often a burden, and for money which none can hold long?"

"Where have you come from that you ask these things?"

"I came over the hill this morning from a cottage just outside the world, and so I have no share in the world. I am just a spectator. But what does it all mean—the hate and the love, the joy and sorrow, the for ever seeking for happiness that must for ever turn to woe in the end?"

"Surely we should be content to take our share of work, and sorrow, and pain; we that take the world's life, and light, and shelter, and sunshine, shall we bear nothing in return?" the woman said in surprise.

"And money? Does money bring you happiness that you seek for it, and bear so much for its sake?"

"Seldom enough, dear, unless it finds other things to keep it company. There is nothing so overrated in all the world as money," the woman said.

"Why do so many seek it?"

"I cannot tell, dear lassie, for I never had it, or desired it; but some is necessary, and all should be willing to work for their share of it, but more than this I cannot understand. Why it is so precious and so difficult to win, where so many are willing to work for it, is one of the strange things one had to think about. There are many better things than money; it is a thousand pities so much good time is wasted in seeking it."

"And why do people desire to work; is it for honour?"

"The best workers think only of their work," the woman answered, "and whether it will be good for the world and in itself, or of what it will do for others, not of what it will do for themselves."

"And love—"

"Ah," the woman said quickly, "out of good love and good work has the world grown up; from them and through them we possess all good things. To love well and to work well are the two things to desire in life, for all other things are in their gift. To the lovers and the students we owe all things."

"But the world is not made up of these, dear mother; there are the soldiers, and the lawgivers, and many others."

"They have been lovers and students first."

The girl did not ask how this might be, for she thought of the words the painter had quoted, "For whatever a man loves he can create, and the work of his hands is that in which his soul delighteth," and dimly she was beginning to understand.

"Why do people desire to do good work for the world which they hardly know and have scarcely seen?" she asked.

"The world is ourselves," the woman answered; "it is the thing we make it, and we can all help to choose what manner of thing it shall be for those who come after us. Even the least of us can help to root out sin, and to make unkindness strange, and some one life better because ours has been. Oh! my dear," she cried passionately, "if I could but hope that you and I may think this, and know it before the day comes when our hands shall be folded, and only our work shall say that we have lived—" But the girl looked on still wondering.

"How did you come to think and know all these things?" she asked.

"I have been alone so long," the woman answered, "just sitting by the fire thinking. But why are you going? Stay a little longer if you will, lassie."

"It is a long way over the hills," the girl answered, "and I must go home to the cottage." As she spoke she looked back longingly at the little town, and at the smoke rising up from the houses in which the people rejoiced, and sorrowed, and worked, and lived out their simple lives. Then suddenly she looked up at the woman.

"Good-bye, dear mother," she said. "It is a strange thing, but I would give the world to put my arms round your neck and kiss you just once."

"And why not?" the woman asked, gently.

"I cannot," the girl answered; "something holds me back. I am just a spectator and have no part in the world, and cannot understand the things for which it cares so much."

"But why is that?"

"Oh, mother, I have no heart, and I live outside the world and have no share or part in it; it joys and sorrows alike pass me by and are never mine," and she started on her way.

"No heart!" the woman said sadly. "Ah, poor lassie! then the world must indeed be a riddle of which you have for ever missed the answer."

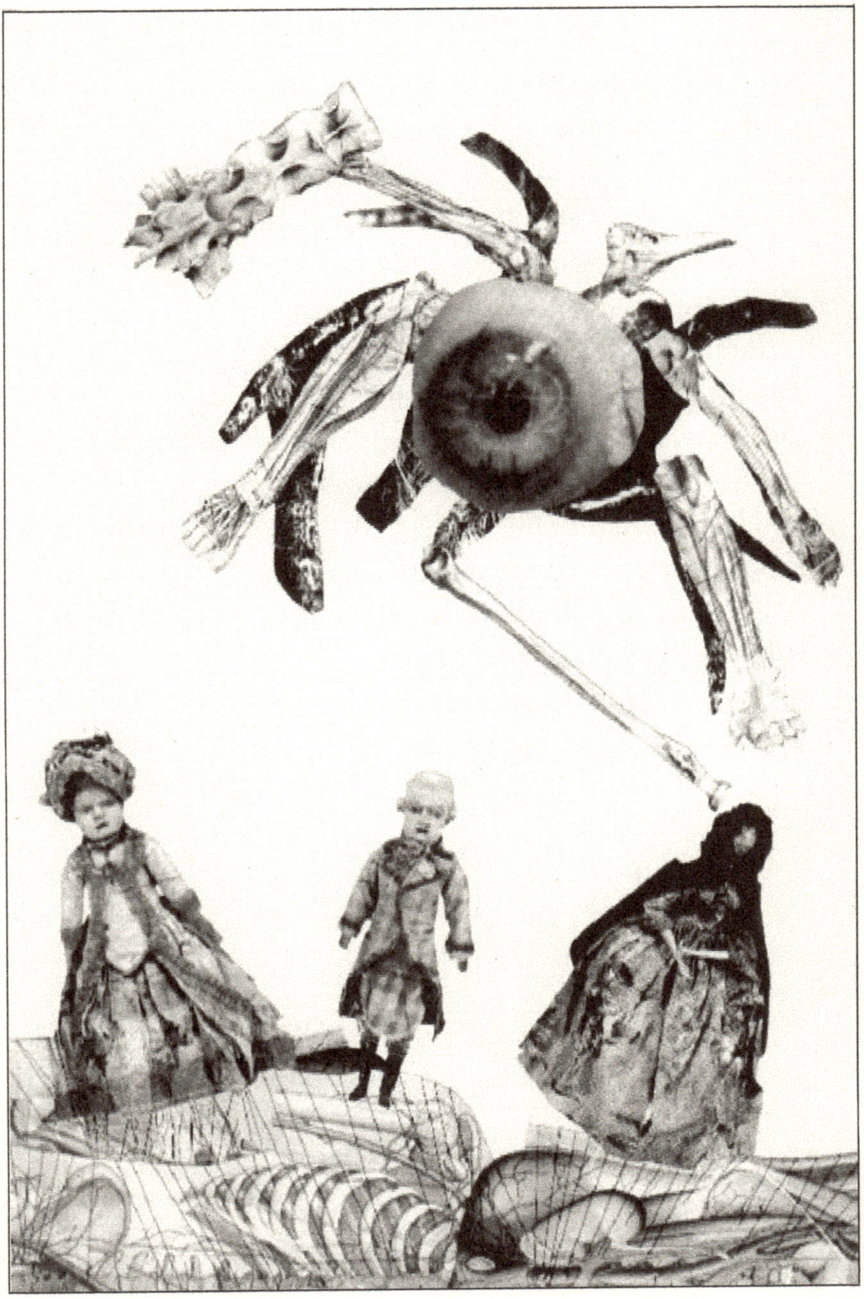

THE WHITE RABBITS

ALL the white rabbits but two, my dears,
All the white rabbits but two,
Away they all sailed in a cockle-shell boat,
Painted a beautiful blue.
All the white rabbits so snowy and sleek,
Away they went down to the shore;
Little they thought, so happy and meek,
They'd never come up from it more.
Oh, the white rabbits they wept and they sobbed,
Till the boat it shook up in the sails;
Oh, the white rabbits they sobbed and they shook
From their poor loppy ears to their tails.
Away they all sailed to a desolate land
Where never a lettuce-leaf grew,
All the white rabbits but two, my dears,
All the white rabbits but two.

THE POOR LITTLE DOLL

IT was a plain little doll that had been bought for sixpence at a stall in the market-place. It had scanty hair and a weak composition face, a calico body and foolish feet that always turned inwards instead of outwards, and from which the sawdust now and then oozed. Yet in its glass eyes there was an expression of amusement; they seemed to be looking not at you but through you, and the pursed-up red lips were always smiling at what the glass eyes saw.

"Well, you are a doll," the boy said, looking up from his French exercise. "And what are you staring at me for is there anything behind?" he asked, looking over his shoulder. The doll made no answer. "And whatever are you smiling for?" he asked; "I believe you are always smiling. I believe you'd go on if I didn't do my exercise till next year, or if the cat died, or the monument tumbled down." But still the doll smiled in silence, and the boy went on with his exercise. Presently he looked up again and yawned.

"I think I'll go for a stroll," he said, and put his book by.

"I know what I'll do," he said, suddenly; "I'll take that doll and hang it up to the apple tree to scare away the sparrows." And calling out, "Sis, I have taken your doll; I'm going to make a scarecrow of it," he went off to the garden.

His sister rushed after him, crying out, "Oh, my poor doll! Oh, my dear little doll! What are you doing to it, you naughty boy?"

"It's so ugly," he said.

"No, it is not ugly," she cried.

"And it's so stupid, it never does anything but smile, it can't even grow, it never gets any bigger."

"Poor darling doll," Sis said, as she got it once more safely into her arms, "of course you can't grow, but it is not your fault, they did not make any tucks in you to let out."

"And it's so unfeeling. It went smiling away like anything when I could not do my French."

"It has no heart. Of course it can't feel."

"Why hasn't it got a heart?"

"Because it isn't alive. You ought to be sorry for it, and very, very kind to it, poor thing."

"Well, what is it always smiling for?"

"Because it is so good," answered Sis, bursting into tears. "It is never bad-tempered; it never complains, and it never did anything unkind," and, kissing it tenderly, "you are always good and sweet," she said, "and always look smiling, though you must be very unhappy at not being alive."

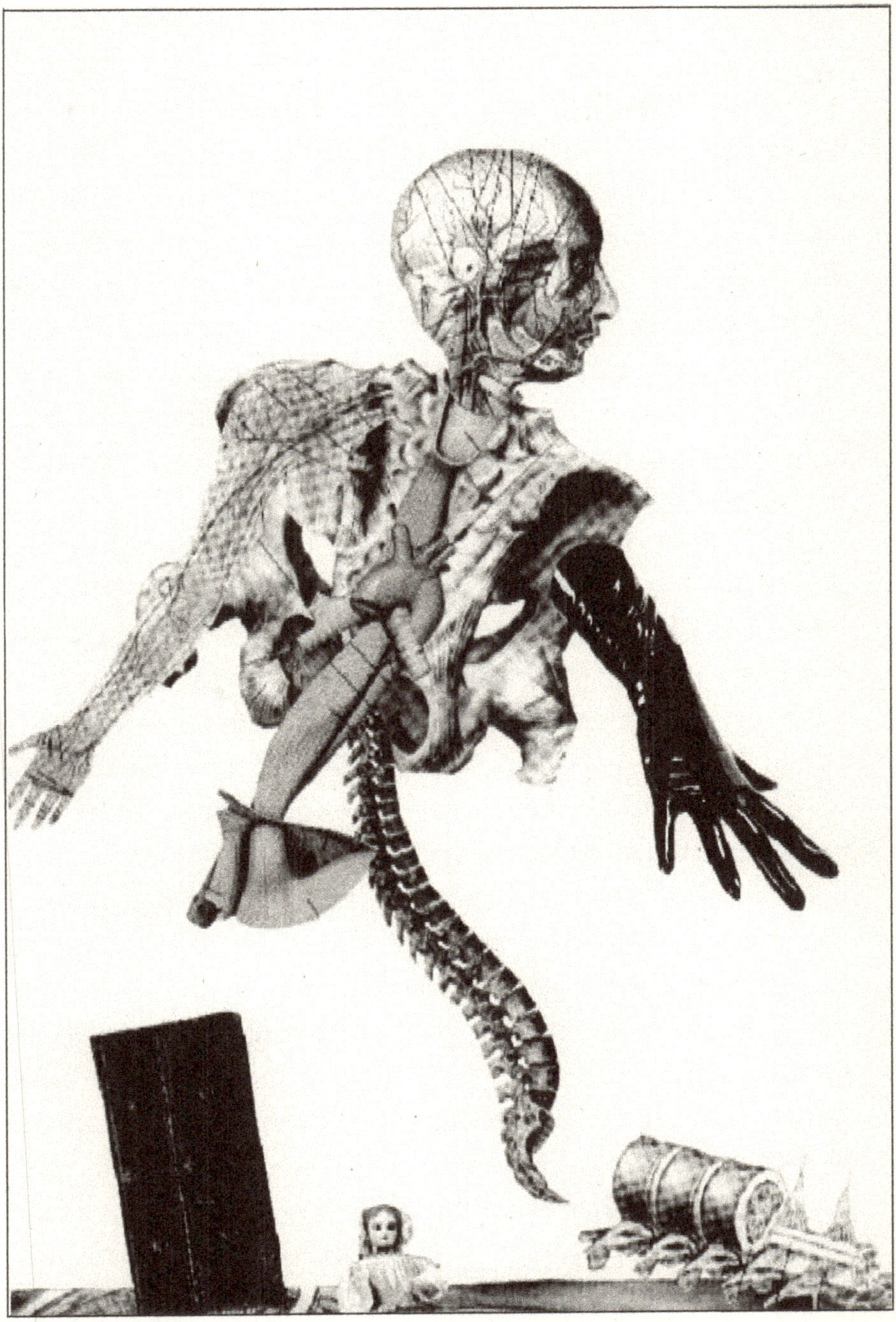

THE COBBLER'S CHILDREN

LONG years ago, my children, all through a dreary afternoon, a child sat in a garret working a sampler. Do you know what a sampler is? It is a bit of canvas on which are worked in cross-stitch some words, and now and then some little pictures. Long ago children were always taught to make them, so that when they became women they might know how to mark their table-cloths and pillow-cases and all the linen of the house, for in those days no tidy housewife had thought of writing her name in ink upon her belongings.

The child's brother was busy at the other end of the garret making a table. At Christmas time a great lady sent him a box of tools; so with some bits of wood his uncle the carpenter had given him he set to work to make her a little table, just as a mark of his gratitude, and to show her how useful the tools would be and how well he meant to work with them. And all the time he was cutting and fitting and measuring the little bit of wood, he was thinking of a book his father had once read to him. The book was written by a wise man, and the wise man had said that he who made the first perfect thing of its kind, no matter how small or simple the thing might be, had worked not merely for himself but for the whole world. He left off for a moment to wonder how this might be, and to think how grand a thing it was to work for the world. "It is a beautiful place," his father said on the day they had read the book together, "and a grand thing to think we have all of us the making of its furniture." Then the boy looked up at the window and at the shoemaker's bench that stood by it, and at an unfinished shoe, a little child's shoe, that was on the bench. "Father takes so much trouble to work well," he said to himself. "He often says that when one does well, one does some good to the whole world, for one helps to make it better; and that when one does badly or does wrong, one does it to the whole world and helps to make it worse than one found it. But," he added, "that cannot be so always. How, for instance, can the whole world know about a little shoe?" Suddenly he looked at his sister and noticed that the tears were stealing down her face, though she tried to hide them, and went bravely on with her sampler, working the figures that made her name and age thus;

SARAH SHORT
AGED 7 YEARS

He watched her and wondered. "If she works her sampler well, will it be good for the whole world?" And then he saw her tears again, and in a moment it seemed as if, of their own accord, his arms had twined round her neck.

"What is the matter?" he asked softly. "You, dear little sister, why are you grieving?"

"Daddy is so ill," she sobbed. "He will never be well again."

"I will love you for him when he is gone," he said. "I will take care of you just as he did.

"Oh, but I wish I could do something for him, because I love him," she cried.

The boy was silent for a few minutes, and stood thinking of all that their father had been to them. Then he said —

"We can't do anything for him now, but we will do things all our lives for him."

Then, while the children stood still close together, a woman entered. "You may come and see your father," she said. "You must tread softly; he is very ill." She looked round the room and saw the chips of wood upon the floor.

"I put the room tidy; you needn't have made such a mess," she grumbled; "I am tired enough." But the boy only heard her as if in a dream, and as if in a dream thought, "I will gather up all the bits by and by, and put the room neat and straight;" and then with soft steps and grave faces the brother and sister went to their father. He was lying on a little bed in the back garret. The children looked round at the whitewashed walls, then up at the little shelf of books above their father's head, then down at their father's face.

"My lass, is that you?" the cobbler said. "And what have you been doing?"

"I have been making this," she answered, and held up the sampler.

"And I have been making the little table," the boy said, answering his father's look; "it is a deal of trouble to get the bits to fit in and lie flat."

"Never mind the trouble, dear lad," the cobbler said gently, looking up at his boy's face; it always told him what was in the boy's heart just as the hands of a clock told him the time that ticked and ticked repeated; "it's because you are sorry a bit to-day you can only do a thing as well as it can be done—that is all the great men do."

"It's no use wasting his time over that table; it is sure to be covered by a cloth," the woman said. "It would do just as well if he were quicker about it," and she left the room. She was a lodger in the same house with the cobbler, and was often puzzled at his ways.

When she had gone, the cobbler turned to his son again. "Don't heed her, lad," he said. "Do your best; do it, lad, don't dream of doing it—good work lives for ever. It may go out of sight for a time; you mayn't see it or hear of it once it leaves your hand; you may get no honour by it, but that's no matter; good work lives on; it doesn't matter what it is, it lives on." And then, tired out, the cobbler closed his eyes and slept—so sweet a sleep, my children, that he never knew waking more....

The children were weary of sitting alone in the twilight. They had nothing to say to each other; they could not see to work, and the sister's eyes ached with crying, and the boy's heart ached with a still sorer pain.

"Let us go to the garden," he said; and hand in hand they went down the stairs, treading softly and slowly lest they should wake the cobbler from his sleep. They sat on the stone steps that led to the garden—an untidy garden, in which nothing grew save a little creeper planted in a painted wooden box. They looked at the creeper; they could dimly see the tendrils struggling to grow up and up just a little way towards the garret window. They wondered if it would grow as high as the shoemaker's bench in the front room, and they thought of the little shoe their daddy had begun to make for the child whose name they did not know. The stars came out one by one; the little sister's eyes filled with tears when she saw them, for it seemed to her that they had changed since she had seen them last, or else that she knew them better. They looked so soft and kind, as if they saw her and were sorry, perhaps as if they loved her just a little bit; and oh, they looked so wise, as if in that great far-off from which they shone all things were known and understood.

"Dear brother," she whispered, "I wonder if they see the little shoe, and Daddy's face and Daddy's books just above his head?"

"I can't tell," the boy answered softly, "but I think they know about them."

"Perhaps they knew Daddy loved us," she whispered again.

"Perhaps they did," he answered with a sigh, and then he said suddenly, "We have so many things to do; we must make a great many things and send them into the world, because he loved us."

"Wouldn't it have mattered about them if he had not loved us?" she asked.

"Oh yes, it would have mattered, he answered; "but I don't think we could have done them, love makes one so strong; it helps one to do and to bear so many things."

"Yes," she said softly, as they turned to leave the garden, "we must make the world a great many things and tell it Daddy sent them." She saw the wind stir the creeper in the painted box, and she said to herself, "Perhaps the little leaves can hear," and as she stood on the top of the steps looking up at the sky once more before she followed her brother into the house, she thought, "Perhaps the dear stars know."

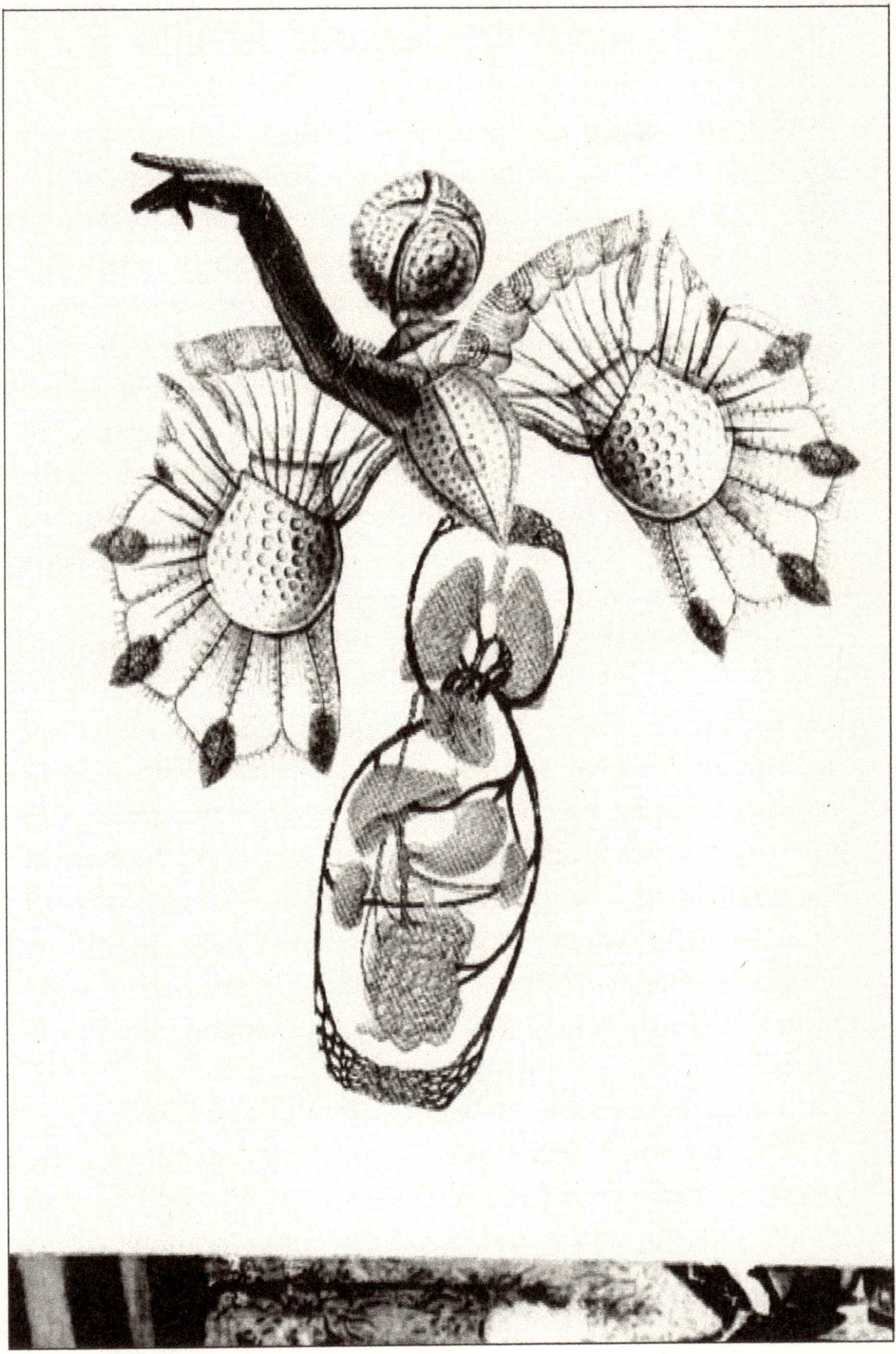

ROUND THE RABBIT HOLES

THE corn was growing up ever so high, and the poppies were red between. At the end of the cornfield there was a stile, and the boy sat on it watching the sun sink lower and lower into the west. "It is looking down on some wonderful city," he thought; "it sees the faces of the men and women glad to welcome it, and ready to work in the new light day, while for us there is only the night. It is a fine thing to be the sun; how grand it would if one could journey on and on in front of it, with the day for ever before one and the night for ever behind!" He heard the children's voices in the distance calling to him, and he answered, "I am here, I am here; come and sit by me." And they came, saying —

"Tell us a story, tell us of the things you will someday do."

"Someday," he said with a sigh, "someday perhaps I shall journey to the strange city to which the sun goes at night. It must be a wonderful city, for, when the great gates in the west open for the sun to pass in, all the sky reddens at the sight of its beauty. Some day when I journey there I shall make all manner of things. I want to make them," he added, and sighed again, "for my father's sake and for my little sister, who is far away in the town waiting for news of them."

"When do you mean to begin?" the children asked.

"I do not know yet. I have to work all day now for my uncle, and when it is over my hands are tired, and I have so much to think about; besides, I can make nothing yet so well as I mean to make it. I like to sit and dream of the days that will come; they will all come, but it's long to wait."

"How long have you been waiting?"

"Ever since Daddy died." he answered.

"Tell us about him." they said, though they had heard many times before. They were never tired of listening to the strange boy that had come to the carpenter's. "Tell us about him and about the little sister;" and the children gathered closer round him, and the tall girl with the pink apron, whose eyes seemed to know some strange language her lips had not yet learnt to speak, drew up closer than the rest, so that she might lose no word of what he said.

"Nurse me," the little one said. Then the girl gathered the little one of three years old upon her lap, and sat on the lower step of the stile, and looked up at the boy's face while he spoke.

"Daddy used to make shoes and mend them," the boy said; "and he and the little sister and I lived in the garret at the top of a house in the town. In the evening, when Daddy had done his work, he used to sit and tell us stories: he told us about all manner of things, of all we must do, and of how the great men were those who did things as best they could be done. It makes one long to do things well so much; I will never do them badly, that is why I am waiting he added softly.

"But one has to try one's 'prentice hand," the mother said. She had come to seek her children, but the boy had not noticed her. "One can but do one's best," she added sadly, "or maybe one gets no time for anything, and goes away as useless as one came." But the boy did not heed her, and went on—

"The little sister used to sit and work, for a woman in the house taught her how to sew, and she kept all the place neat, and tried to do the things that would please Daddy, though she was only seven years old; and sometimes while Daddy worked at the bench she would sing songs to him."

"Ah, the little doers are better than the great dreamers," the mother said.

"And what did you do?" the girl with the pink apron asked.

"I always had so much to think about," he answered; "and then once my uncle came to see us, the same uncle with whom I am living now, and he saw the box of tools which the lady, for whose crippled child Daddy made shoes, had given me, and he sent me some bits of wood, and I set to work to make things. Daddy told me to be satisfied only when I had done my best, and to count all else as nothing, 'for when one did well,' he said, 'one did it for all the world.'"

"But one can get one's hand in by working for those about," persisted the mother.

"Go on," said the children, impatiently; "tell us about the little sister."

"She is with the lady who sent me the tools, learning how to do many things."

"And where is the little table you made?" they asked, though they all knew.

"It is in the great lady's drawing room," he answered with a smile. "Someday I shall make a much better one, but

I am waiting till I know more, and have thought of some grander way to work than I know now....The night that Daddy died," he went on suddenly, "my sister and I went into the garden; we saw the stars come out, and we looked at a little creeper planted in a wooden box; it was growing up against the wall," and suddenly he stopped.

"Go on," they said.

"But that is all," he answered. "The little sister went to the great lady, and I came here, and am working for my uncle the carpenter, and am waiting—the rest is in my heart."

"Tell us what is in your heart," they said.

"I do not know yet," he answered. "One does not find out all at once."

"Now take us to see the rabbit holes," the children said, "and tell us all about the rabbits." So the boy rose to do as they wished, and the mother cried—

"Do not keep them out long; and see the little one does not fall," she added, speaking to the girl with the pink apron.

"I will carry the little one," the boy said, taking her in his arms. The girl with the pink apron walked beside him, and the rest followed, talking among themselves as they went along. All down the cornfield they went, and over the gate with the padlock on it into the wood. Then soon they turned aside from the pathway and went in among the shadiest trees. The ground was thick with brake and briar and under wood, the nuts hung green on the branches above them, the blackberries were almost ripe on the bushes as they passed by.

"They are here," he said, and he stopped by a tree that grew at the farthest side of the wood, close to the hedge that parted off the hayfield. They could see the schoolhouse across the field, and the church, and they remembered the gate that stood close by the church and led to the village. The schoolmaster had stacked his hay, and the ricks were there right across the field, compact and well-shaped and comfortable-looking, ready for the winter; the children thought of the haymaking, but it was always nicer to be in the woods than in the fields. In the fields the green was only under their feet, but in the woods it was all about and above them, as if the sweet world wrapped them round and filled them with its beauty, till their hearts brimmed over with content. The tree by which the boy had stopped was so tall and shady, it seemed as if the top that looked at the sky must be a long way off. "Here they are," he said. "I have never seen the rabbits, but I often think about them." The children went forward one by one and peeped in the holes, and the little one looked down at them, holding the boy tighter while she did so. Then they all stood in a group waiting for the boy to speak.

"Tell us what they do when they come out of their holes," they said.

"I don't know," the boy answered. "I have never seen them."

"What do you think they do?"

"I think that when the wood is still, and not a sound or voice or footstep can be heard, they peep out, and if they hear and see no one, they come out gaily and play about among the ferns and grass until they are tired, and they give little, short, quick runs, stopping to nibble a leaf or to listen to some strange sound, or else they stay still a while just to drink in, without knowing anything about them, the sweetness of the air, and the brightness of the sun, and the silence of the shade, and the little cool breeze that steals among the leaves and passes on."

"And what do they do at night?"

"Ah, at night they have fine fun. They scamper across the hayfield, running ever so swiftly, with their ears put back and their little tails shaking, till they find their way into the schoolmaster's garden, and they eat the cool, crisp lettuce leaves, and play at hide-and-seek among the cabbages, and then they scamper to the hayfield again, and wander by the hedge back to the wood, and there they play about till the long gray dawn grows lighter and lighter."

"Surely you would like to see them?" the girl with the apron said.

"No," said the boy. "I can think about them. I should not like them better if I saw them, and they might go and I should miss them. The things on thinks about stay unless one sends them away, and they never change unless one's self changes first."

"How did you learn to think?" the girl asked curiously.

"Daddy used to talk to me," answered in surprise; "and it's just as if he talked to me still, or had written things down in a book. All the people we love teach us to see and hear."

"Do you love the people you don't see?" she asked, "for you love the things you don't see."

"Oh, yes," he said, "I love all people, they are so good," he added. "I have heard there are bad people, but I never knew any. All people have hearts, and if one makes for them one always finds them. But come," he said, "we must go home." And the children, not understanding what the boy and girl were talking about, turned silently round towards the gate that led to the cornfield. The little one's head drooped on the boy's shoulder, for she was tired. "You dear little one," he whispered; "my sister was small like you once, and I used to carry her in my arms down to the garden, and sit on the stone steps with her, waiting for the stars."

"The stars are in the sky already," he girl said.

"Yes," answered the boy, and he whispered to the little one—"The stars are coming out. They will all be out soon; they are shining down upon the little garden in the town, and the creeper is growing up to meet them; it will touch the garret window on its way."

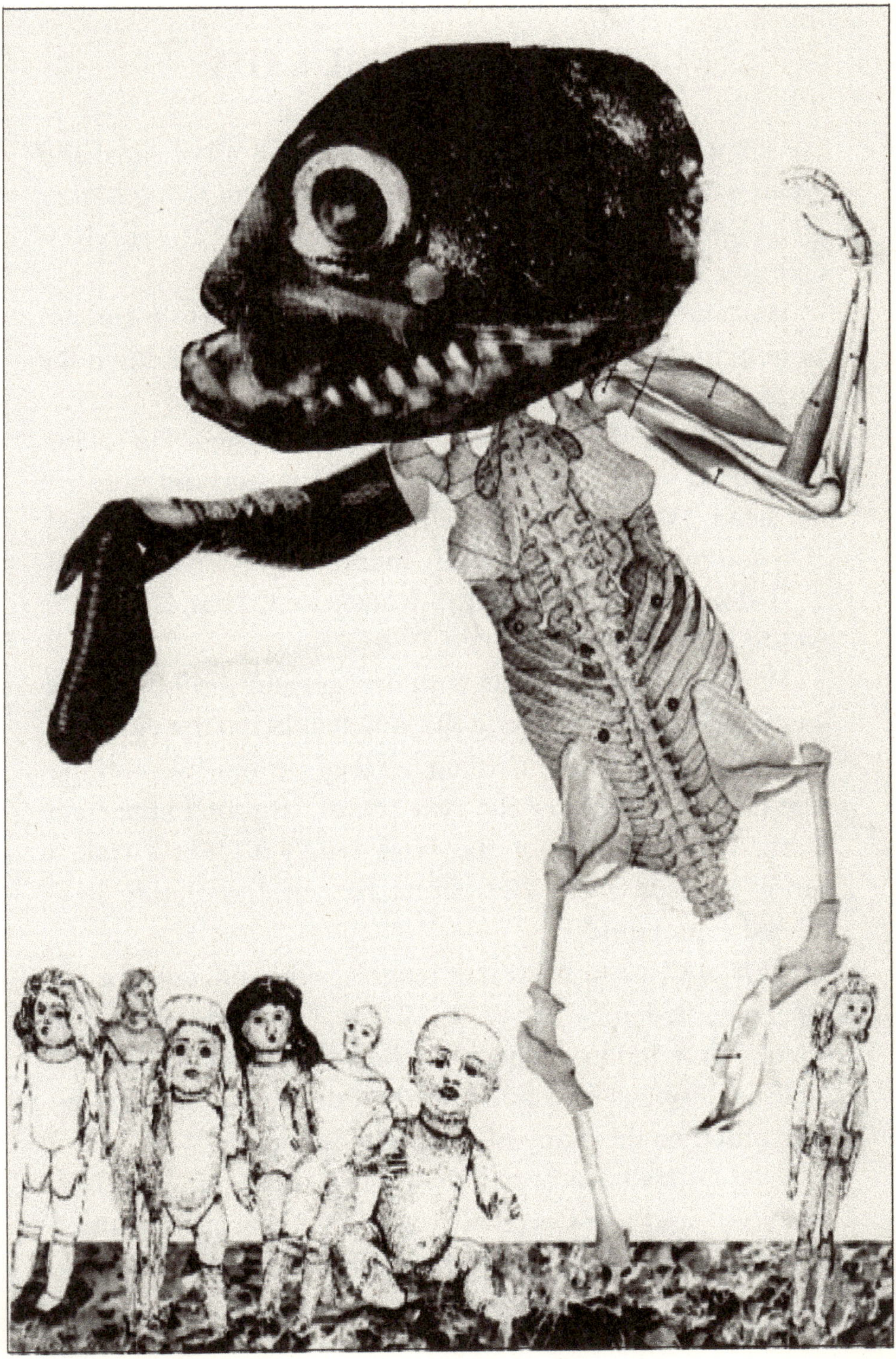

THE BEAUTIFUL LADY

THE woods were all white with the blossom of April and green with the coming of May. The larks were flying higher and higher watching for the swallows afar off—surely it was time they had started on their way?

The children went to the woods, but they were not singing for joy as usual; they followed the tall girl down the pathway.

"Janet," the little one said, "see, that is where the rabbit-holes used to be," but Janet only nodded, and did not turn her head. "We never saw the rabbits," the little one added. "Do you think the lad ever saw them?"

"I don't know," the tall girl answered; "but I think he would have told me if he had."

They filled their baskets with flowers and went out of the wood, and sauntered along the lane that led to the village.

"Janet," the little one asked, as they passed two cottages that had been built just the year before, "is it there the crazy woman lives?" One of the boys laughed. "She's such a funny mad woman." But before he could say more Janet turned round quickly.

"It is only a bad heart that laughs," she said; and the boy was ashamed in a moment. "Come," she added, "let us cover her window-ledge with flowers." And eagerly the children stopped and piled up the flowers on the window-still, and then they tapped at the window-pane.

"The fairies have been," they cried; "see what they have left you," and went on their way. They heard the window opened and the woman's voice singing:—

> *"And oh, my heart is sad to-day,*
> *And oh, 'tis full of sorrow,*
> *For sweet my love is far away,*
> *And won't be home to-morrow.*
> *And won't be home to-morrow-day,*
> *And won't be home — "*

Then she stopped with a little cry of joy, and the children knew she had found the flowers.

The tall girl's heart gave a leap when she heard the woman's cry, and she clasped the little one's hand more tightly. "Ah, poor dear!" she thought, "the lad at the carpenter's would have known how to comfort you with his talk of the strange lands your son's eyes never saw, and the lad knew only in his heart."

All down the lane the children went — past the lilac-trees just bursting into bloom, past the farmhouses, — they could hear the grunting of the pigs, and the rattle of the milking-pans the dairy-maid was washing as they passed by, — and on toward the village. But when they came in sight of their mother's cottage they stopped suddenly, for there, waiting by the door, stood a grand carriage.

"Janet," they whispered, afraid to speak aloud, "it must be the beautiful lady." They stood still, not liking to go on and wondering what to do. But the little one looked up and said —

"I do want to see the beautiful lady." So they gathered courage and went slowly on to the cottage, and one by one they shyly entered in at the door, curtseying as they did so, for the beautiful lady sat by the fireplace talking to the mother. The little one was glad the china dog she won off the Christmas-tree stood upon the mantelpiece, for half a dozen times did the beautiful lady look up at it; and for ever afterwards it seemed to have a remembrance of her, though it only told it to the little one.

Janet had learnt all manner of things from the carpenter's lad — to love books and the histories of far-off lands, and all manner of strange stories; and in the evening she talked to the children of all she knew. So when they saw the beautiful lady they thought of the fairy-queen who loved a mortal man and took him off to fairyland, and they fell to wondering if this could be she. She had blue eyes and soft golden hair, which was twisted all round her head, till it looked just like a crown. She had surely listened while Thomas the Rhymer played upon his harp, they thought: and perchance she knew where the three roads met and one branched off to Elfinland. She had taken her gloves off, and they saw that on her little finger she wore a gold ring with a green stone set in it. Perhaps when she was tired of earth, they thought, she turned it round three times and found herself in fairyland once more. And while they thought all this, and stood in a group staring at her, they heard the clicking of the harness on the horses, and knew that really she was no fairy at all, but just the beautiful lady who had come to live in the big house beyond the bridge; but of course she might have been the fairy-queen — it seemed so odd that she was not. She turned and looked at the children with her sweet blue eyes, and then she said — it seemed a wonderful thing to hear her voice —

"I have come to ask your mother about a boy who lived in this village. He was a cobbler's son; I know his sister." Then all speaking together the children answered —

"The strange lad at the carpenter's."

"Did you know him?" the lady asked.

"Yes, we all knew him," they answered, "but Janet knew him best. He used to take us to the woods to show us the rabbit-holes. They are not there now, and we never saw the rabbits. He used to tell us stories about the strange countries, and of all the things he meant to do."

"And while he was thinking of all the great ends he would gain he forgot to make any beginning," the mother said. She was a stern woman, but her voice was sad while she spoke. "He was always dreaming," she added, "and while he was dreaming his hands were folded."

Then the beautiful lady sighed but made no answer, for she thought how many of us are like the cobbler's son, longing to climb great heights, looking up at the far-off light, yet standing still the while; and as for the things we see and do in dreams, — should we not most of us travel far and wide and achieve great things indeed, if we could but tack our hands and feet on to our fancies?

The tall girl who had known the boy so well, went forward a step.

"He worked hard all day," she said gently; "he did all that was given him to do. It was only in the evening that he read books and thought of the strange countries and told us of his dreams and of all he meant to do. Once he made a little table," she began, but before she could say more the beautiful lady interrupted her.

"I know," she said, "it is my brother's home far away in India. It was my mother's, and because it was made so well she once sent it down to the schoolhouse, so that all the village boys might see it, and know how well a cobbler's little son could work."

"Yes, yes," the children cried, eagerly crowding up close round the beautiful lady; "oh, go on and tell us more, we know he made a little table."

"And as it was coming back from the schoolhouse," she went on, "the man who carried it let it fall, and a little piece of wood that was not so firmly glued as the rest fell from the under part, and we saw that beneath it had been written: *'Daddy's lad made this table, and sent it into the world with his love,'* and we all thought much about these words, and how the cobbler's little son had put one thing at least that was well done into the world. And when my brother went away to India, he asked my mother for the little table, and he took it with him; and in one of his letters he said it always seemed to him more like a living thing with a human voice than a bit of furniture."

"He was a clever lad," the mother sighed, her stern face relaxing a little.

"He used to tell us about all manner of things," the children said; "we were never tired of hearing."

"But it was all waste of time," the mother said.

"No, dear mother," the tall girl answered gently, "I do not think so, for we all loved him, and somehow after he came we all loved each other more." Then the mother's eyes suddenly filled with tears.

"His heart was stronger than his hands," she said to the beautiful lady, "and what the girl says is true; he taught us to love better, but he never knew it. And he loved the children, and the birds, and the bats, and the bees, and the sunshine, and the flowers that grew in the woods. It was wonderful how he loved them all."

"And they loved him back again!" the tall girl said eagerly.

Then the beautiful lady gently touched the mother's arm that was brown and bare, and said softly —

"He did not only dream, dear woman, and there are some dreams far better and sweeter than any waking."

"But the pity of it is that we live our lives awake," the woman said. "But the poor lad," she added sadly, "he sleeps on just by the pathway between the church and the schoolhouse."

"Come and see," the little one cried, "oh dear beautiful lady, come and see!" and almost before she knew it, the beautiful lady had risen from her seat and taken the little one by the hand and left the cottage; and tall girl walked by her side, and the children followed in a group. So they went on to the place where the carpenter's lad slept well.

It was close by the pathway, just as the mother had said, so that if he did not sleep too soundly, he could hear the children's voices singing in the schoolhouse, or the patter-patter of their feet when the church clock struck the hour, at which the schoolhouse door opened wide, and they came joyfully forth and hurried away to their homes.

"He is here," said the children softly, and they stood still, while the beautiful lady looked down at the grass growing wild and tall above him.

"We told the man not to cut the grass often," they whispered; "for when it grows up high it seems like the woods, and he was always so happy in the woods."

"There are some wildflowers growing among the grass," the beautiful lady said.

"Ah, yes," the tall girl answered, "we don't know how it is, but there are always flowers among the grass above him; we think sometimes that perhaps they are his little dreams coming through."

ROUND THE TEA-TABLE

A NICE little party we're seated at tea,
The dollies all seem very glad,
Save the poor little thing who is leaning on me;
I fear that she feels rather bad;
Poor limp little thing! she wants a back-bone,
She's only just made up of rag.
There's little Miss Prim sitting up all alone,
And the Japanese looks like a wag.
Now what shall we talk of, my own dollies fair?
And what shall we give you for tea?
That queer little thing with the short frizzy hair,
Why does he keep looking at me?
My sister and I we will sing you a song
Before we get up from the table;
It shall not be sad, and it shall not be long
We'll sing it as well as we're able.

SONG

The darkness is stealing all over the place,
The flowers are weeping for sorrow,
The daisy is hiding its little round face,
The sun has gone seeking to-morrow.
So while you are seated all round the tea-table,
Please join in the chorus as well as you're able;
O! sing! sing away for your life.

CHORUS
It's time to cut off the dicky birds' noses,

> *Time to cut off the dicky birds' noses,*
> *It's time to cut off the dicky birds' noses,*
> *So bring me the carving-knife.*

The darkness is hiding the birds on the trees,
The thrushes are weary of singing,
A strange little rumour is borne on the breeze
Of Summer the swallows are bringing.
So while you are seated all round the tea-table,
Please join in the chorus as well as you're able;
O! sing! sing away for your life.

> *CHORUS*
> *It's time to cut off the dicky birds' noses,*
> *Time to cut off the dicky birds' noses,*
> *It's time to cut off the dicky birds' noses,*
> *So bring me the carving-knife.*

The Summer is stealing all over the place,
The wind is all scented with roses,
The dear little birds are all flying a race,
On purpose to give us their noses.
So while you are seated all round the tea-table,
Please join in the chorus as well as you're able;
O! sing! sing away for your life.

> *CHORUS*
> *It's time to cut off the dicky birds' noses,*
> *Time to cut off the dicky birds' noses,*
> *It's time to cut off the dicky birds' noses,*
> *So bring me the carving-knife.*

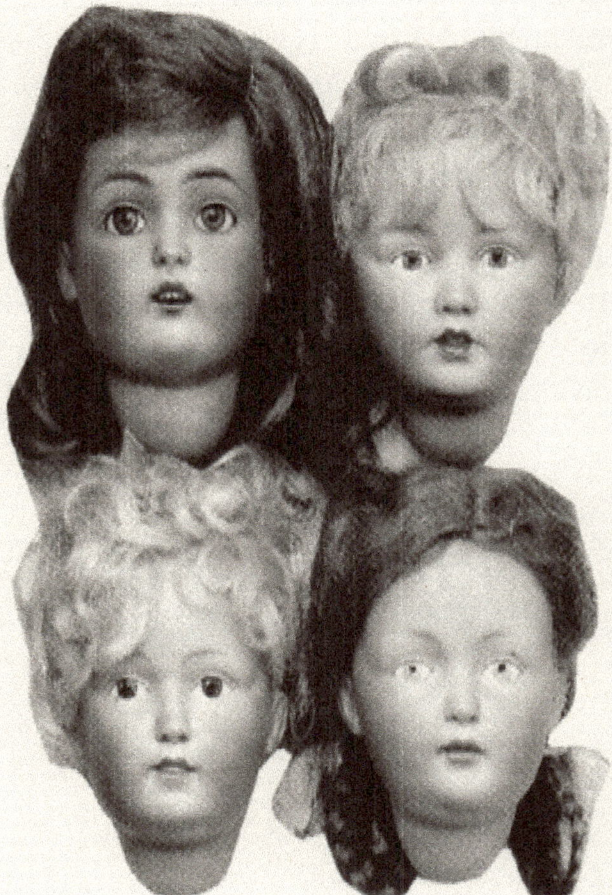

THE BROKEN HORSE

THEY were all very sad, and the girl in the pink frock was crying bitterly, for they had been to the woods, and on the way home the wooden horse had fallen over on one side and broken off his head.

"Don't cry so, pray don't cry so," the little one said, as she knelt down in front of her sister, and tried to kiss her.

"And oh, sister," said the brother, "it would have been far worse if he had lost his tail too. Besides, perhaps he does not mind much; it is not as if he were alive."

"Ah, yes," sobbed the tall girl. "But when you are as old as I am you will know that it is a terrible thing to lose your head, even if it is only wooden."

MASTER WILLIE

THERE was once a little boy called Willie. I never knew his other name, and as he lived far off behind the mountain, we cannot go to inquire. He had fair hair and blue eyes, and there was something in his face that, when you had looked at him, made you feel quite happy and rested, and think of all the things you meant to do by-and-by when you were wiser and stronger. He lived all alone with the tall aunt, who was very rich, in the big house at the end of the village. Every morning he went down the street with his little goat under his arm, and the village folk looked after him and said,

"There goes Master Willie."

The tall aunt had a very long neck; on the top of it was her head, on the top of her head she wore a white cap. Willie used often to look up at her and think that the cap was like snow upon the mountain. She was very fond of Willie, but she had lived a great many years and was always sitting still to think them over, and she had forgotten all the games she used to know, all the stories she had read when she was little, and when Willie asked her about them, would say,

"No, dear, no, I can't. Remember; go to the woods and play."

Sometimes she would take his face between her two hands and look at him well while Willie felt quite sure that she was not thinking of him, but of someone else he did not know, and then she would kiss him, and turn away quickly, saying,

"Go to the woods, dear; it is no good staying with an old woman."

Then he, knowing that she wanted to be alone, would pick up his goat and hurry away.

He had had a dear little sister, called Appleblossom, but a strange thing had happened to her. One day she overwound her very big doll that talked and walked, and the consequence was quite terrible. No sooner was the winding-up key out of the doll's side than it blinked its eyes, talked very fast, made faces, took Apple-blossom by the hand, saying,

"I am not your doll any longer, but you are my little girl," and led her right away no one could tell whither, and no one was able to follow.

The tall aunt and Willie only knew that she had gone to be the doll's little girl in some strange place, where dolls were stronger and more important than human beings.

After Apple-blossom left him, Willie had only his goat to play with; it was a poor little thing with no horns, no tail and hardly any hair, but still he loved it dearly, and put it under his arm every morning while he went along the street.

"It is only made of painted wood and a little hair, Master Willie," said the blacksmith's wife one day.

"Why should you care for it; it is not even alive."

"But if it were alive, anyone could love it."

"And living hands made it," the miller's wife said.

"I wonder what strange hands they were; take care of it for the sake of them, little master."

"Yes, dame, I will," he answered gratefully, and he went on his way thinking of the hands, wondering what tasks had been set them to do since they fashioned the little goat. He stayed all day in the woods helping the children to gather nuts and blackberries. In the afternoon he watched them go home with their aprons full; he looked after them longingly as they went on their way singing.

If he had had a father and mother, or brothers and sisters, to whom he could have carried home nuts and blackberries, how merry he would have been. Sometimes he told the children how happy they were to live in a cottage with the door open all day, and the sweet breeze blowing in, and the cocks and hens strutting about outside, and the pigs grunting in the styes at the end of the garden; to see the mother scrubbing and washing, to know that the father was working in the fields, and to run about and help and play, and be cuffed and kissed, just as it happened. Then they would answer,

"But you have the tall lady for your aunt, and the big house to live in, and the grand carriage. To drive in, while we are poor, and sometimes have little to eat and drink; mother often tells us how fine it must be to be you."

"But the food that you eat is sweet because you are very hungry," he answered them, "and no one sorrows in your house. As for the grand carriage, it is better to have a carriage if your heart is heavy, but when it is light, then you can run swiftly on your own two legs." Ah, poor Willie, how lonely he was, and yet the tall aunt loved him dearly.

On hot drowsy days he had many a good sleep with his head resting against her high thin shoulders, and her arms about him. One afternoon, clasping his goat as usual, he sat down by the pond. All the children had gone home, so he was quite alone, but he was glad to look at the pond and think. There were so many strange things in the world, it seemed as if he would never have done thinking about them, not if he lived to be a hundred.

He rested his elbows on his knees and sat staring at the pond. Overhead the trees were whispering; behind him, in and out of their holes the rabbits whisked; far off he could hear the twitter of a swallow; the foxglove was dead, the bracken was turning brown, the cones from the fir trees were lying on the ground. As he watched, a strange thing happened. Slowly and slowly the pond lengthened out and out, stretching away and away until it became a river a long river that went on and on, right down the woods, past the great black firs, past the little cottage that was a ruin and only lived in now and then by a stray gipsy or a tired tramp, past the setting sun, till it dipped into space beyond.

Then many little boats came sailing towards Willie, and one stopped quite close to where he sat, just as if it were waiting for him. He looked at it well; it had a snow-white sail and a little man with a drawn-sword for a figurehead.

A voice that seemed to come from nowhere asked

"Are you ready, Willie?"

Just as if he understood he answered back, "Not yet, not quite, dear Queen, but I shall be soon. I should like to wait a little longer."

"No, no, come now, dear child; they are all waiting for you." So he got up and stepped into the boat, and it put out before he had even time to sit down. He looked at the rushes as the boat cut its way through them; he saw the hearts of the lilies as they lay spread open on their great wide leaves; he went on and on beneath the crimson sky towards the setting sun, until he slipped into space with the river.

He saw land at last far on a-head, and as he drew near it he understood whither the boat was bound. All along the shore there were hundreds and hundreds of dolls crowding down to the water's edge, looking as if they had expected him. They stared at him with their shining round eyes; but he just clasped his little goat tighter and closer, and sailed on nearer and nearer to the land. The dolls did not move; they stood still, smiling at him with their painted lips, then suddenly they opened their painted mouths and put out their painted tongues at him; but still he was not afraid. He clasped the goat yet a little closer, and called out, "Apple-blossom, I am waiting; are you here?"

Just as he had expected, he heard Apple-blossom's voice answering from the back of the toy-town, "Yes, dear brother, I am coming." So he drew close to the shore, and waited for her. He saw her a long way off, and waved his hand.

"I have come to fetch you," he said.

"But I cannot go with you unless I am bought," she answered, sadly, "for now there is a wire spring inside me; and look at my arms, dear brother," and pulling up her pink muslin sleeves, she showed him that they were stuffed with sawdust. "Go home, and bring the money to pay for me," she cried, "and then I can come home again." But the dolls had crowded up behind, so that he might not turn his boat round.

"Straight on," cried Apple-blossom, in despair; "what does it matter whether you go backwards or forwards if you only keep straight when you live in a world that is round?"

So he sailed on once more beneath the sky that was getting grey, through all the shadows that gathered round, beneath the pale moon, and the little stars that came out one by one and watched him from the sky. I saw him coming towards the land of storybooks. That was how I knew about him, dear children. He was very tired and had fallen asleep, but the boat stopped quite naturally, as if it knew that I had been waiting for him. I stooped, and kissed his eyes, and looked at his little pale face, and lifting him softly in my arms, put him into this book to rest. That is how he came to be here for you to know. But in the toy-land Apple-blossom waits with the wire spring in her breast and the sawdust in her limbs; and at home, in the big house at the end of the village, the tall aunt weeps and wails and wonders if she will ever see again the children she loves so well.

She will not wait very long, dear children. I know how it will all be. When it is quite dark tonight, and she is sitting in the leather chair with the high back, her head on one side, and her poor long neck aching, quite suddenly she will hear two voices shouting for joy. She will start up and listen, wondering how long she has been sleeping, and then she will call out

"Oh, my darlings, is it you?" And they will answer back, "Yes, it is us, we have come, we have come!" and before her will stand Willie and Apple-blossom. For the big doll will have run down, and the wire spring and the sawdust will have vanished, and Appleblossom will be the doll's little girl no more. Then the tall aunt will look at them both and kiss them; and she will kiss the poor little goat too, wondering if it is possible to buy him a new tail. But though she will say little, her heart will sing for joy. Ah, children, there is no song that is sung by bird or bee, or that ever burst from the happiest lips, that is half so sweet as the song we sometimes sing in our hearts a song that is learnt by love, and sang only to those who love us.

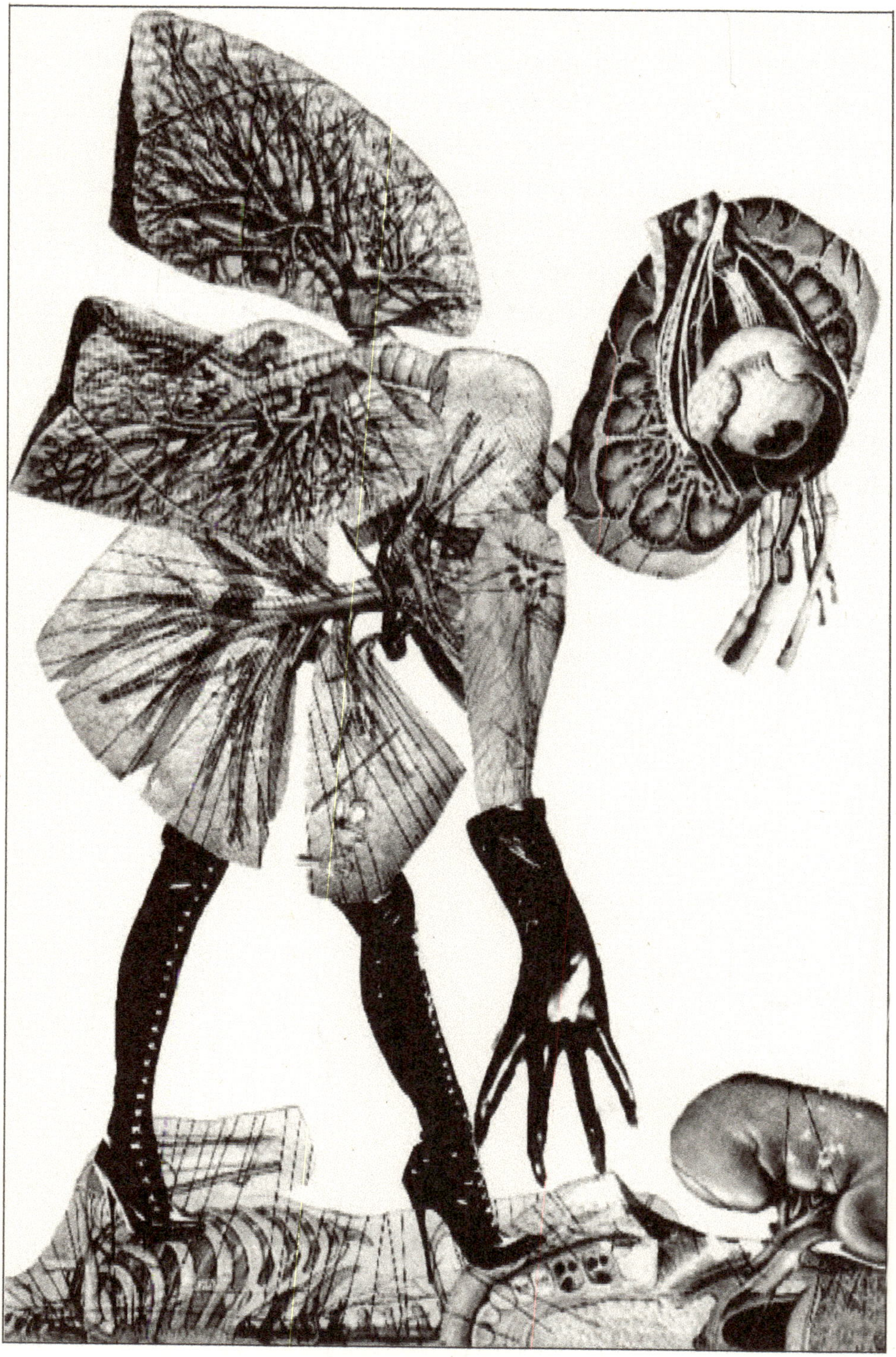

THE WOODEN HORSE

"COME and have a ride," the big brother said.

"I am afraid," the little one answered; "the horse's mouth is wide open."

"But it's only wooden. That is the best of a horse that isn't real. If his mouth is ever so wide open, he cannot shut it. So come," and the big brother lifted the little one up, and dragged him about.

"Oh, do stop!" the little one cried out in terror; "does the horse make that noise along the floor?"

"Yes."

"And is it a real noise?"

"Of course it is," the big brother answered.

"But I thought only real things could make real things," the little one said; "where does the imitation horse end and the real sound begin?"

At this the big brother stood still for a few minutes.

"I was thinking about real and imitation things," he said presently. "It's very difficult to tell which is which sometimes. You see they get so close together that the one often grows into the other, and some imitated things become real and some real ones become imitation as they go on. But I should say that you are a real coward for not having a ride."

"No, I am not," the little one laughed; and, getting astride the wooden horse, he sat up bravely. "Oh, Jack, dear," he said to his brother, "we will always be glad that we are real boys, or we too might have been made with mouths we were never able to shut."

IN THE MOONLIGHT

HE picked a buttercup, and held it up to her chin.

"Do you like butter" he asked.

"Butter!" she exclaimed. "They are not made into butter. They are made into crowns for the Queen; she has a new one every morning."

"I'll make you a crown," he said. "You shall wear it tonight."

"But where will my throne be?" she asked.

"It shall be on the middle step of the stile by the cornfield."

So when the moon rose I went out to see. He wore a red jacket and his cap with the feather in it. Round her head there was a wreath of buttercups; it was not much like a crown. On one side of the wreath there were some daisies, and on the other was a little bunch of blackberry blossom.

"Come and dance in the moonlight," he said; so she climbed up and over the stile, and stood in the corn-field holding out her two hands to him. He took them in his, and then they danced round and round all down the pathway, while the wheat nodded wisely on either side, and the poppies awoke and wondered. On they went, on and on through the corn-field towards the broad green meadows stretching far into the distance. On and on, he shouting for joy, and she laughing out so merrily that the sound travelled to the edge of the wood, and the thrushes heard, and dreamed of Spring. On they went, on and on, and round and round, he in his red jacket, and she with the wild flowers dropping one by one from her wreath. On and on in the moonlight, on and on till they had danced all down the corn-field, till they had crossed the green meadows, till they were hidden in the mist beyond.

That is all I know; but I think that in the far faroff somewhere, where the moon is shining, he and she still dance along a corn-field, he in his red jacket, and she with the wild flowers dropping from her hair.

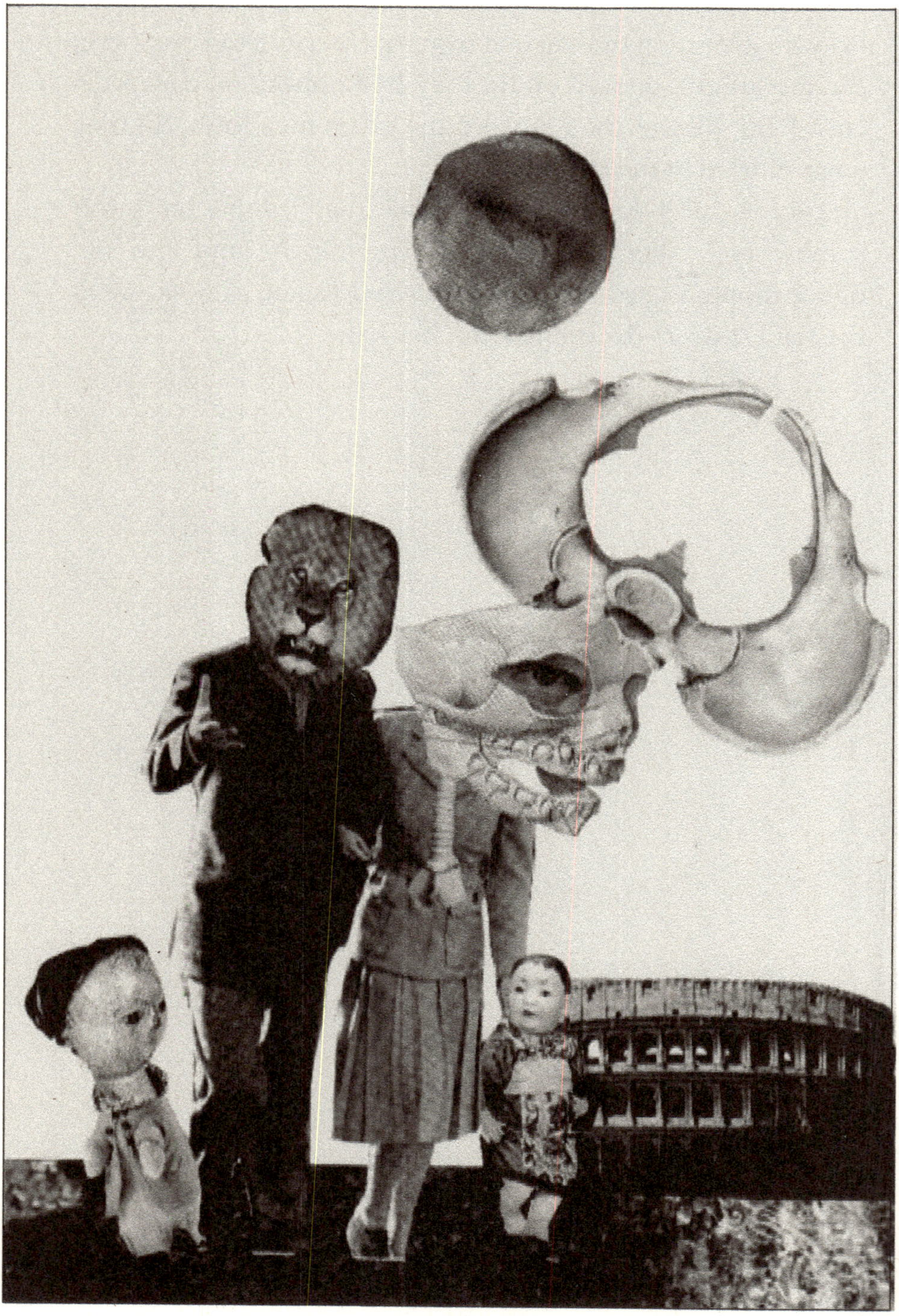

TOMMY

TOMMY was sitting on the bench near the end of the lane. By his side was a basin tied up in a cotton handkerchief; in the buttonhole of his coat there was a sprig of sweet-william.

The girls from the big house came and stood still in front of him, staring at him rudely, but he did not speak.

"Tommy, are you tired?" they asked.

"Yes," Tommy answered, crossly, "I'm very tired, and father's working in the fields, and I have got to take him his dinner before I go to the fair."

"Why don't the servants take it?"

"Servants!" said Tommy scornfully; "we've no servants. We are not rich people!"

"Wouldn't you like to be rich?" the eldest sister asked, while the two little ones walked slowly round Tommy, looking at the feather in his hat; he had put it there so that he might look smart when he went on to the village.

"No, it's too expensive," said Tommy, shaking his head; "rich people have to buy such a lot of things, and to wear fine clothes, and they can't have dinner in the fields."

"My father has his dinner in a room," said the girl.

"That's because he's rich," answered Tommy, "and people would talk if he didn't; rich people can't do as they like, as poor can."

"And my father lives in a big house," the girl went on, for she was vulgar, and liked to boast.

"Yes, and it takes up a lot of room; my father's got the whole world to live in if he likes; that's better than a house."

"But my father doesn't work," said the girl, scornfully.

"Mine does," said Tommy, proudly. "Rich people can't work," he went on, "so they are obliged to get the poor folk to do it. Why, we have made everything in the world. Oh! it's a fine thing to be poor."

"But suppose all the rich folk died, what would the poor folk do?"

"But suppose all the poor folk died," cried Tommy, "what would the rich folk do? They can sit in carriages, but can't build them, and eat dinners, but can't cook them." And he got up and went his way.

"Poor folk ought to be very kind to rich folk, for it's hard to be the like of them," he said to himself as he went along.

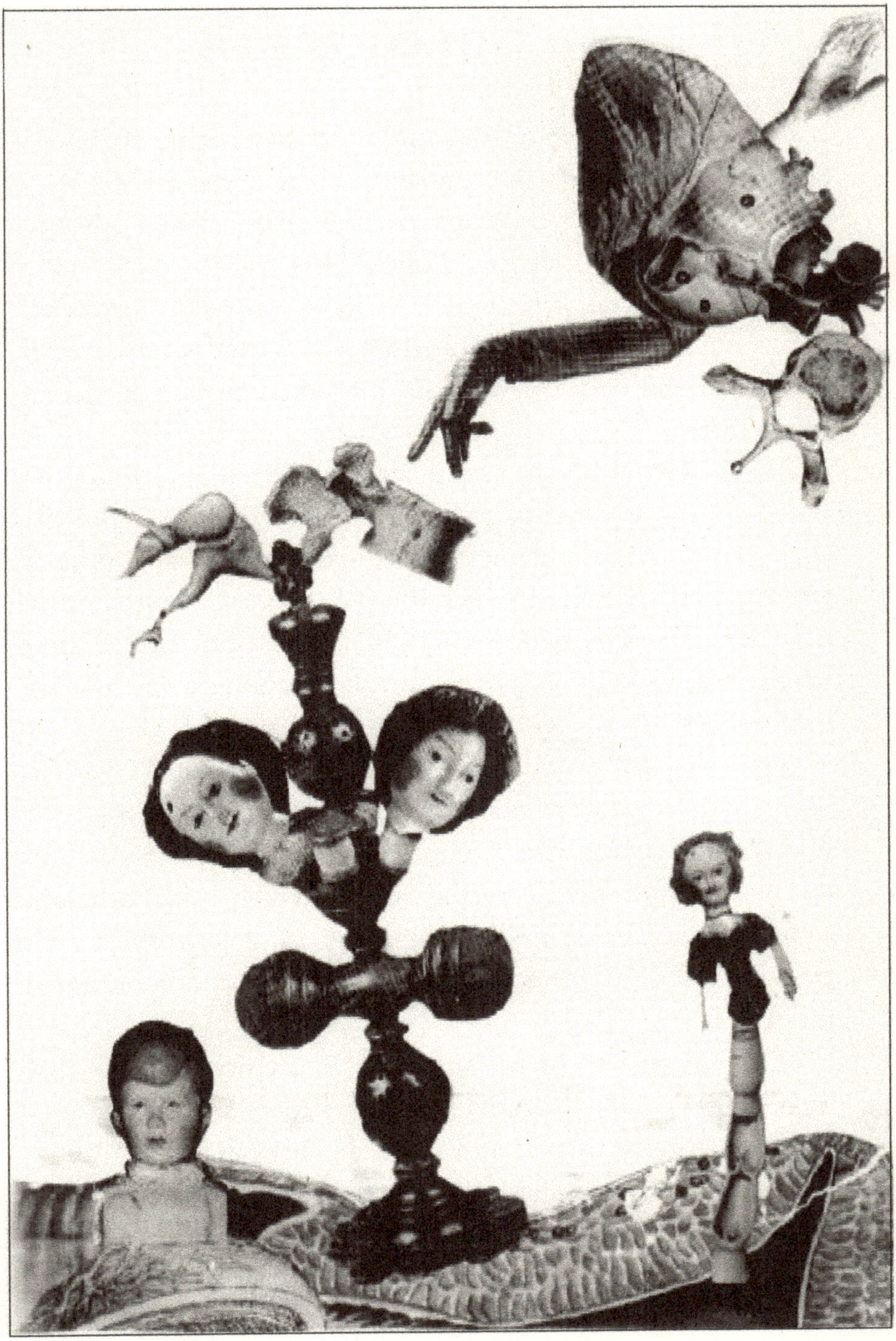

THE IMITATION FISH

IT lived with three or four imitation ducks in a cardboard box, to which there was a glass lid. It was about an inch and a half long, and made of tin; one side was painted a bright red, and the other a deep yellow. At the end of its nose was a very little bit of wire, and this bit of wire sadly puzzled the poor imitation fish. The ducks and the fish were all packed in soft cotton-wool, and placed in a quiet corner of the toy-shop.

The fish would have had a comfortable sleepy time if its nose had not been always longing to touch a strange little stick at the other end of the box. The ducks had no such longing and aching, at which the fist wondered much, until it noticed that they had no tiny bit of wire at the end of their noses, and somehow it could not help connecting this fact with their placid peacefulness.

One day, the ducks and fish and the little stick (which, with the exception of about a third of an inch at one end, was painted a bright red) were all violently disturbed, and the next minute the lid of the box, in which they had slept so long, was quickly pulled open, and a fair little child with golden hair and large grave blue eyes stood looking at them.

"Oh, you pretty ducks!" he cried, in a voice so sweet that the imitation fish longed for a heart to beat at its sound. "Oh, you pretty ducks, and you dear little fish, I will take you home, and you shall swim in the nice cool water." And the lid was gently closed, and the little child carried the box home to a tall house by the sea. "No you shall have a large bath to swim in," the child said, "and you shall be as happy as the day is long."

And then the gay little ducks and the red-and-yellow fish were placed in the cool clear water, and bravely swam upon its surface. Ah, how happy they were, going round and round as the fancy of the child directed, listening to the gleeful voice, and sometimes feeling themselves taken up by the careful fingers, looked at for a moment, and then tenderly placed on the water again!

"Mother," the child asked, "what is the little stick for?"

"It is a magnet," the mother answered. And then she showed the child how to hold it close to the little bit of wire at the end of the fish's nose, and lo! in a moment, the whole of the imitation fish's being seemed satisfied, and it clung to the stick as if the gift of life were in it, or swam swiftly and recklessly after it, as if a whirlwind were behind.

"There is only one fish, mother," the child said presently, taking the stick out of the water, "but there are three or four ducks. Poor little fish! how lonely you must be, with no other—"

Then a voice was heard calling, and the child vanished, leaving the fish and the ducks aimlessly waiting in the bath. Presently the mother came, and lifted them all out, and put them once more into their box.

"The dear child!" she said lovingly to herself; "all things are real to him as yet; even this foolish bit of painted tin he does not dream to be without life or feeling, for he knows nothing of things that are false."

And she placed the box on a shelf, and left the fish wondering greatly at the words it had heard.

The next morning the ducks and the little fish again swam about the bath, and chased the strange stick round and round, while the child laughed with glee, and was happy; but the fish was not so bright as yesterday, for it remembered the words it had heard, and wondered much. And yet the child loved the little fish far more than the placid and contented ducks that troubled themselves not at all about anything.

"Don't be lonely, little fish," the dear voice would say, while the tender fingers put it away in the cotton-wool. "I will come and see you again to-morrow."

One day the little fish heard the child ask —

"Do all the fish live in the sea, mother — in the great sea which is before our windows?"

"All real fish do, my darling," the mother answered.

"And when they are taken out, mother, what then?"

"They die — the real fish do."

And the poor imitation fish feared lest its falseness should be betrayed to the one heart that knowing no falseness, thought it must be real; but the mother said nothing more. And many times that day it was taken from its resting-place, and looked at long and lovingly, and kissed. And once the soft voice said —

"Ah, dear fish! you shall not be lonely long. I will not let you die, because I love you; to-morrow I will take you back to your great home, the sea."

Then the little fish, having learned to love the child, trembled, for how could it bear to leave the one thing that cared for it?

And when the morrow came, the child took the fish once more from its soft little home, and looked at it for a few minutes with sorrowful blue eyes, and then gently carried it away—away from the stick and the imitation ducks and the little cardboard box in which it had lived so long, and out of the house by the sea, which was the child's home.

The sound of the waves came nearer and nearer, and on and on the child went, until at last he stopped at the end of a long pier, beneath which the water rushed and foamed. Then the child looked at the imitation fish again, and kissed it for the last time, while his tears fell upon its red-and-yellow sides.

"Farewell, dear little fish," he said. "You shall never be lonely more, or live in a stupid little cardboard box; you shall go back to your home in the sea, and dwell among others like you. I love you, dear little fish—farewell!" and the child dropped it into the deep water beneath. For one moment the poor little imitation fish dimly saw out of one painted eye the sweet face above, and then the waves tossed it away and away, farther and farther out to sea.

"Ah, dear child," it cried in terrible fear, "your purity has been the ruin of my false self. I was not made for things that were real; now I am indeed lost."

But no one took any notice of the poor toy, and the living fish swam past it with scarcely a glance; even they knew it was a sham; and when the fisherman cast his line into the sea, the hook at the end did not touch or hurt the imitation fish; all around it was heedless of its presence, only the waves went on tossing it day after day, week after week. Sometimes the sunlight came, and the real fish swam into the fisherman's net; but nothing pleased or hurt or harmed the imitation fish—only the waves went on tossing and tossing.

At last, after a long, long time, the waves seemed to be going on and on, always in one direction, and the fish went with them, until at last it was thrown on the shore among the pebbles and seaweed, and the little pools of water that collected between great stones; and the little fish was thankful, for it had escaped from a great loneliness, and the quiet of the shore seemed a blessed thing after the ceaseless tossing of the waves.

How long it lay there it never knew, but one day there was a sudden sound of a voice, and the little fish was lifted up by hands almost as tender as the child's.

"It is so like a toy my darling love!" a voice said; and a great happiness stole over the poor little fish, for he knew the voice of the child's mother. "He had a little fish that pleased him more than all his other toys, but he thought it was real, and threw it into the sea to make it happy," and she raised it to her lips, and kissed it passionately again and again, and bathed it in her tears. Then the little fish was sad, and yet thankful and glad to feel itself going back to the child.

And the mother put it in a soft hiding-place, and looked at it many a time, kissing it tenderly; for the sound of the child's voice was hushed, and the blue eyes that had so lovingly watched the imitation fish watched it never again—grave blue eyes that were closed for evermore.

THE DONKEY ON WHEELS

THERE was once a poor little donkey on wheels. It had never wagged its tail, or tossed its head, or said, "Hee-haw!" or tasted a tender thistle. It always went about, anywhere that anyone pulled it, on four wooden wheels, carrying a foolish knight, who wore a large cocked hat and a long cloak, because he had no legs. Now, a man who has no legs, and rides a donkey on wheels, has little cause for pride; but the knight was haughty, and seldom remembered his circumstances. So the donkey suffered sorely, and in many ways.

One day the donkey and the knight were on the table in front of the child to whom they both belonged. She was cutting out a little doll's frock with a large pair of scissors.

"Mistress," said the knight, "this donkey tries my temper. Will you give me some spurs?"

"Oh, no, sir knight," the child answered. "You would hurt the poor donkey; besides, you have no heels to put them on."

"Cruel knight!" exclaimed the donkey. "Make him get off, dear mistress; I will carry him no longer."

"Let him stay," said the child, gently; "he has no legs, and cannot walk."

"Then why did he want spurs?"

"Just the way of the world, dear donkey; just the way of the world."

"Ah!" sighed the donkey, "some ways are very trying, especially the world's," and then it said no more, but thought of the fields it would never see, and the thistles it would never taste.

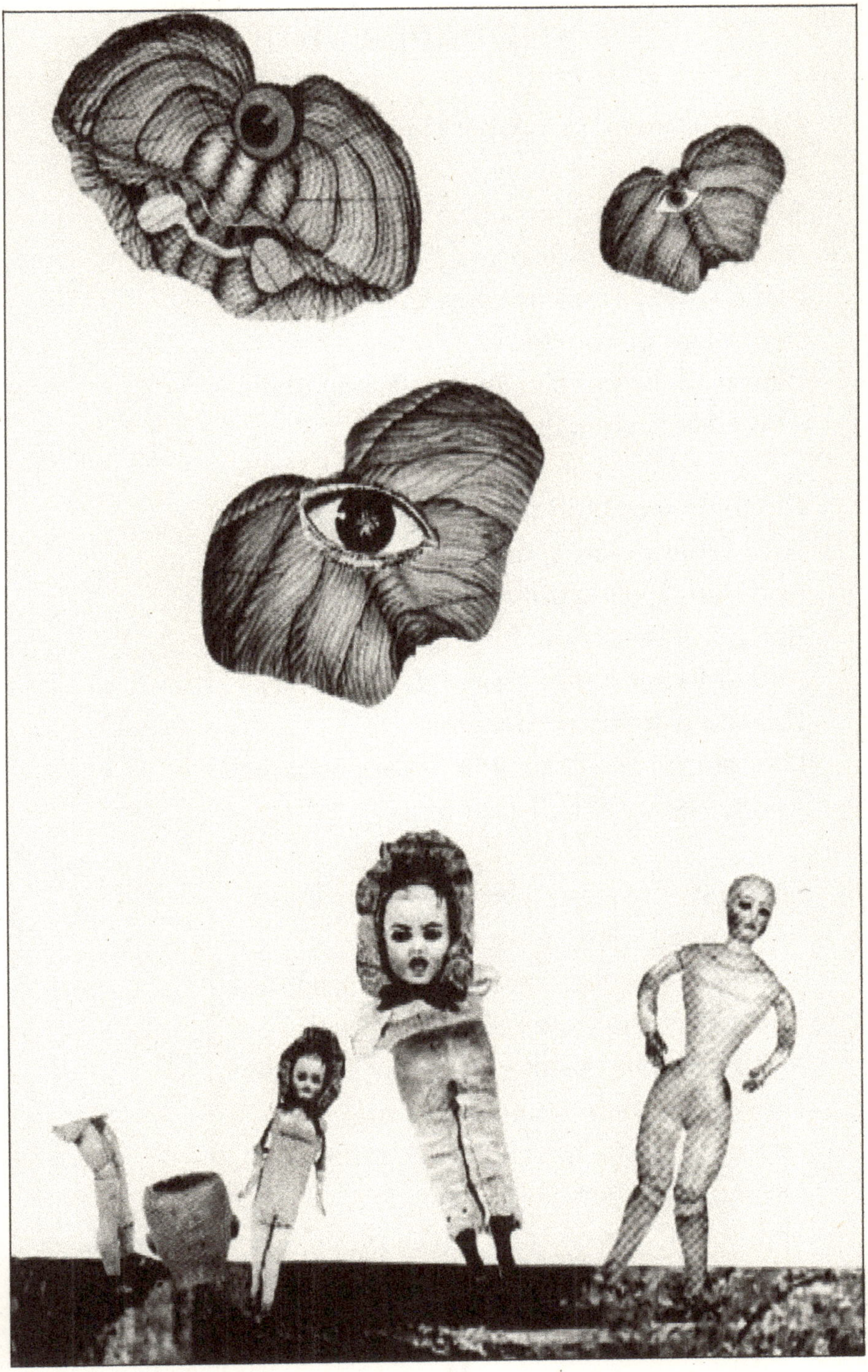

THE PAPER SHIP

I SAILED away in a paper ship,
I sailed away and away,
And never did sailor sail so far,
And never was sail so gay.
I sailed away to an unknown land,
Beyond an unknown sea,
Where all the people were dolls, my dear,
And all of them talked to me.

The town was built of card and paint,
The gardens were made of tin;
And dolls looked out at the windows, dear,
And all of them asked me in.
And dolls sat round on the chairs inside;
They all were dressed so fine;
They stared at a clock that never had ticked,
And was ever at half-past nine.

"What shall we do to be real?" they cried,
"What shall we do to be real?
We none of us feel, though we look so nice,
And talk of the vague ideal."
And all of them seemed to know so much,
But none of them laughed or sang;
And none of the fires had ever a blaze,
And none of the bells e'er rang.
And people walked and talked of life,
And all of them looked so grave;

Yet none of them ever had life, my dear,
Or ever a soul to save.

I fled away to the woods and fields;
The trees were stuck with glue;
And even the sky was false, my dear,
And painted a lovely blue.
And dogs and sheep and cows were there,
And all of them stared at me
With large glass eyes that never had blinked,
And never a one could see.

I sailed away in a paper ship,
Away on an unknown sea;
And all the fishes were hollow, my dear,
And all of them swam at me.

But on and on and on I sailed;
I met a great wet seal,
He looked at me with two dim eyes,
And turned upon his heel.

The strangest sail that never was sailed,
And sight that never was seen —
The sail I sailed in my paper ship, —
The land that never has been.

THE THREE LITTLE RAGAMUFFINS

THEY all stood at the corner of the street looking at the stall with the pine-apples, and at the man who was selling slices for a penny each.

"If I had a penny I would have a bit; I would have the biggest bit there!" said the first little ragamuffin. He was a greedy little ragamuffin, and liked big bits.

"It looks bad to take the biggest; I'd take the fire that came," said the second little ragamuffin.

"I'd take the biggest!" said the third little ragamuffin; "for if I didn't, someone else would think me a fool for leaving it." And then they all went to the rail at the end of the court and turned and whirled and twisted over it and under it and all round about it, until their legs ached and their heads felt dizzy, and the palms of their hands tingled with excitement.

Suddenly, the third little ragamuffin stopped, and sitting astride on the top of his rail, was silent for a few minutes; then he looked at his companions.

"There's Mary Le been to the stall and bought a bit of pine-apple," he said; "shall we go and ask her how she likes it?" And in a moment they had all scampered up to her; but Mary Lee was afraid, and, dropping her pine-apple in the mud, began to cry, and ran home without it. And an old gentleman who was watching them caught the first little ragamuffin and boxed his ears; the second little ragamuffin picked up the piece of pine-apple, and brushing the mud from it with his sleeve, ate it up, and thought how good it was; and the third little ragamuffin went back to the rail alone, and slowly and sadly whirled round it again. Meanwhile his friend was crying bitterly, for his ears had been boxed, and he had had no pine-apple.

"Please, sir," he said to the old gentleman, "we were not doing any harm; we were only going to ask her how she liked it."

"And the consequence was she dropped her pine-apple into the mud."

"Yes, sir, but she ought to have held it tighter; and I didn't get any, though I am very hungry."

"You look fat enough."

"Yes, sir," sobbed the poor little ragamuffin, "mother likes us fat; but it takes a lot of keeping up."

"I daresay it does," the old gentleman said, and, pulling a sixpence out of his pocket, he gave it to the boy. "Here," he said, "take this; but let the lesson I have given you teach you experience. Do you know what experience is?"

"No, sir," answered the ragamuffin.

"It is a thing that youth is eager for, and that age regrets, and that only a fool buys twice; yours to-day bought you a box on the ear."

"And sixpence, please sir." But the old gentleman turned away, and did not hear him. Then the ragamuffin bought six bits of pine-apple and carried them to his friends, and they all three sat in a row on the top of the rail and ate in silence, lest talk should spoil the flavour of a single mouthful. And when it was gone, the first little ragamuffin told his companions all that the old gentleman had said; while they, delighted at the feast they had, whirled round and round the rail for joy. But the first little ragamuffin sat up thoughtfully while he told his story, and pondered over it all.

"You see, Mary Lee, she lost her pine-apple and you ate it, and the old gentleman—"

"He boxed your ears!"

"And gave us sixpence!"

"And then he said it was experience," said the thoughtful ragamuffin.

"Well, we say experience is excellent," answered the two little ragamuffins, whirling round faster and faster; for they had eaten the pine-apple and found it good. But still their friend sat thinking.

"Yes," he said at last, "experience is excellent; but it's best when another fellow buys it."

Meanwhile the old gentleman was walking home, for he had given away his last sixpence; and Mary Lee was sitting in her mother's cottage, crying over her dropped pine-apple.

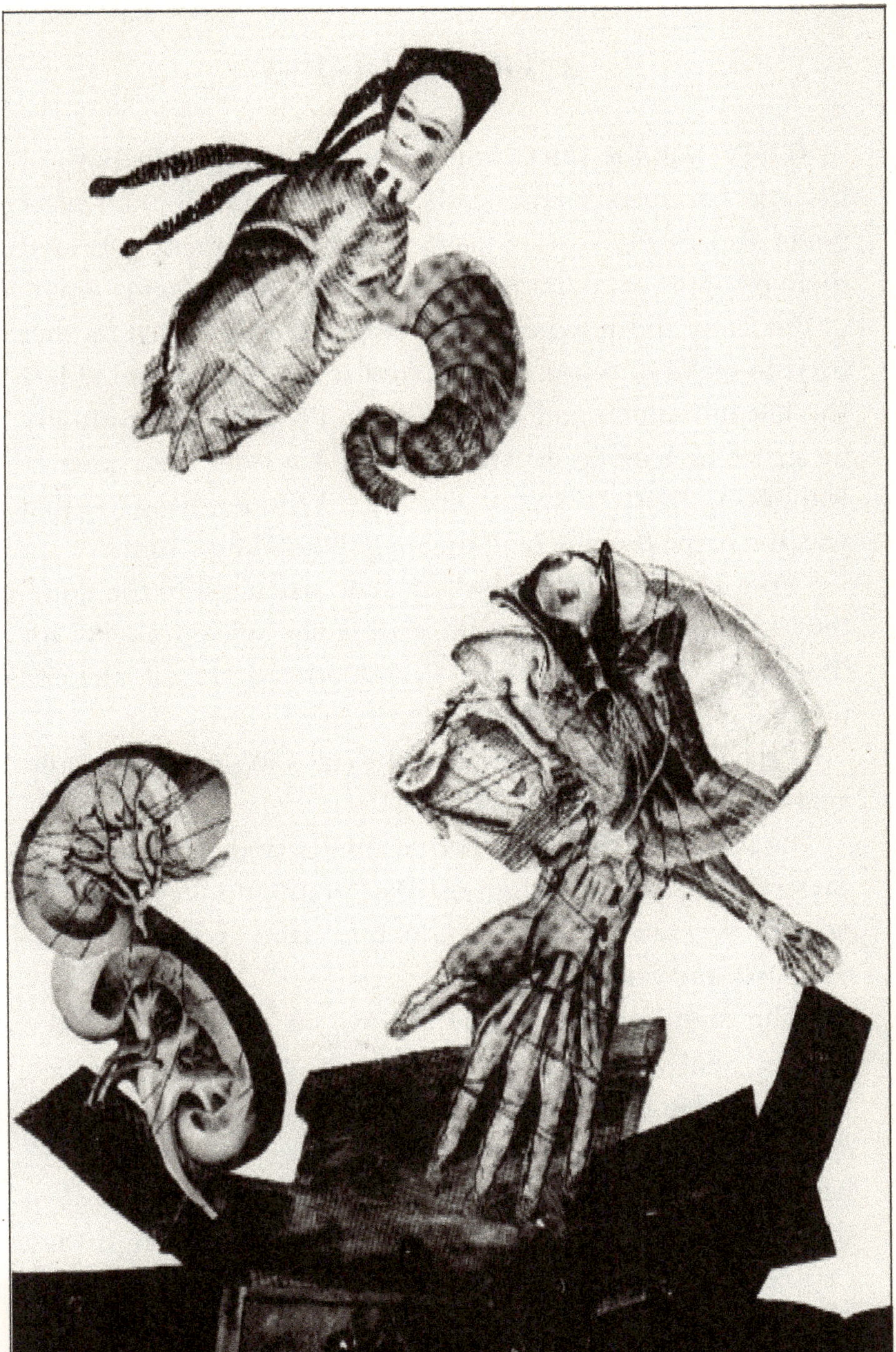

WOODEN TONY

TONY was the idlest boy in Switzerland. Other boys of his age chopped wood, gathered edelweiss, looked after goats and cattle; carried parcels for the strangers, guided them on short expeditions; and earned pence in many ways.

But Tony did none of these things, and when his mother tried to make him useful he looked so frightened that at last she left him alone and let him do as he pleased. Gradually he grew to look quite stupid, as if his wits had gone a-wandering: and he was called the "Wooden-head" – that was the name by which all the neighbours knew him.

"Poor little Wooden-head! He's no use at all to the you," they said to his mother; and at this she waxed angry, for though she often called him Wooden-head herself, she did not like to hear others do so.

"Perhaps he thinks more than he cares to say," she would answer.

"But he never tells of what he thinks; and a thinker who says nothing is like a signpost that points no way, and has nought written on it to guide him who looks up," old Gaspard said one morning.

"The signpost was made before the writing, and the talking that is worth hearing only comes after much thinking. He'll tell us enough someday" the mother answered. But though she spoke up bravely she was sad at heart. "I love thee dearly, my little son," she said. "I love thy pale face and wide open eyes, looking as though they expected to see Heaven's door creak on its hinges so that thou mightest know what the heavenly city was like; but who besides will care for thee if thou art stupid? And if thou art useless who will want thee? Even thy father gets impatient." Tony turned from the faggot that was beginning to crackle and merrily lick with its long flames the black soup-pot hung over it.

"Could I be with thee and yet far off?" he asked. "I long to be far off."

"Dear mercy!" his mother exclaimed. "But why dost thou want to be far off, Tony?"

"Then would I be little and could lie in thy arms; and none would want me to do the things I cannot do and forget to do."

"But how would being far off make thee little, my son?"

"All the people are little far off," he answered. "I often watch the strangers come down the pathway from the big house. They grow bigger and bigger as they come near; they pass the door and go on by the gorge, getting smaller and smaller till they are as little as the figures in the wood that my father cuts away in the winter. When they return they grow bigger and bigger again as they come near. Yes—I want to be very little and far off."

"My son, thou art a fool," his mother said. "Is thy father even smaller, dost thou think? It is only the distance that makes the strangers seem as thou hast said; if thou drew near them thou wouldst see that they had neither grown smaller nor larger." But Tony shook his head and would not understand.

"They are little to me," he said. "I would like to go away and be little to thee again, and then thou wouldst not be always asking me to do this thing and that, and be angry at my forgetting. There are so many things in my head that come before my eyes and make my hands useless."

"Thou art no good if thou art useless," his mother sighed. "All things have a reason for staying in the world, and the reason for the young and strong is that they are useful." But Tony answered only, --

"Someday I will go far off and be very little," and went to the sunshine and sat down on his little stool by the door. Presently he began to sing a song learnt in some strange fashion unknown to any near him, as a solitary bird might learn from its own little lonely heart.

"Ah, dear child," his mother said sadly as she listened. "He is no fool in spite of his talk, or if he be one, then his voice is sweeter than the wisest; there is not room for an evil thought anywhere within sound of it. While I listen to him I could even forgive Gaspard's wife for getting the fine linen to be washed for the English lady. It was a small thing to quarrel about."

But you do not know yet where Tony lived. In the summer his home was far up a high mountain in Switzerland. Beneath was a valley abounding in little meadows and winding pathways that had at one end a waterfall. The waterfall fell over a mountain side and was like a dream forgotten before waking-tine, for though the spray went down and down, it never reached the bottom, but scattered itself in the sunshine and was lost. Tony used to watch the falling water, and try to feel as he imagined it felt--caught by the breeze and carried away in its arms. Sometimes he could almost fancy himself journeying with it--on and on, till he lost all likeness to himself, and, meeting the great winds, he became a part of them, and swept over the far-off sea. All about the valley and here and there on the mountains were the chalets or dark wooden houses of the peasants. Some were built on piles, so that when the storms and floods came the herdsmen and their beasts might still keep themselves dry; and some had heavy stones on their roofs, so that the winds might not blow them away. When Tony was very little, and before he had seem the builders at work, he thought that the piles were wooden legs on which the chalets had walked up in the darkness and stillness of the night, and that the two little windows in most of their fronts were eyes with which they had looked out to guide themselves. He often wished that he could see them staggering step by step upward along the zig-zag pathways. When he grew older it was almost a grief to know that human hands had built them on the mountain and in the valley, and that they would stay where they first rose till the winds and rains had done their worst. There was a little heap of rubbish on one side of the mountains; he had often wondered what it meant, but at last he knew, and then he stood looking at it and thought sadly of the children crouching over the fire, while the herdsman watched the sweeping storm gather to shatter their home and leave it in the past.

Just above his father's chalet was a big stone house, called the Alpine Hotel, where strangers came and stayed in the summer. The strangers talked among themselves in a language Tony did not understand, and were curious about the country round, professing to love it much, and day after day they walked over little bits of it. It seemed odd to Tony that they should travel from far countries to see the things he had lived among all his life--just the hills and valleys, the snow and the edelweiss, the sunshine and the infinite stillness. Was it really for these that the strangers came? He wondered for these that the strangers came? He wondered sometimes what more might be in the distances beyond his home, and in what strange forms the great world stretched itself. Yet he did not trouble often about either the strangers or the world they came from, but silent and lonely let the days and nights slip by as one that swims with but just enough movement to keep himself from drowning. So Tony seemed to swim through time, and to find each day as difficult to remember from the one that went before or came after it as he would have it to tell one mile of sea from another. Sometimes he wondered if the strangers were people easy to break, or to kill, or to get lost, for though they never ceased praising the beauty of the mountains, yet they were afraid to go alone up the steep paths or on the snow-plains that he could have wandered over in his sleep. But it was good that they had so little courage, for they gave his father money to show them the mountains ways, to carry their food, and pull them across the little precipices and crevasses that Tony scarce noticed, to cut steps on the sheer ice to which his feet clung surely, to take care of them altogether, those foolish strangers who professed to love the mountains and yet were afraid to be alone among them. All day long while his father was away Tony stayed in the chalet watching his mother scrub and clean and wash, and make the soup ready for his father at night. Or he would sit by the doorway, listening to the falling avalanche, and letting the warm sun fall on his closely-cropped head. Happy Tony! The trees made pictures and he saw them, the wind blew and he understood: surely he belonged to the winds and the trees, and had once been a part of them? Why should he trouble to work? Vaguely his heart knew that not to work as his father and mother worked had the journeyed into the world from the mists beyond it. Had he not been very little once when he set out on that first journey? Some day, when he had done his resting on the mountain, he would go on into the distance, and be very little once more. And there were, besides, other thoughts than these that came into his heart, for he and nature were so near akin--thoughts of which those about him knew nothing; but he had few words with which to talk; even the easy ones of daily life his lips found difficult to use.

When the evening came, and the soup was eaten, he stood by the doorway, listening to his father's stories of what the strangers had said and done. Sometimes when they had been niggardly or very silent or the day a disappointing one, his father would be cross and grumble at the soup, or reproach Tony for being idle; but his mother always took his part.

"Nay, nay, do not be hard on him," she would say. "Now he is as one called too soon, before his sleep has satisfied him, and his dreams overtake his waking hours. Let him get his dreaming done, and he will rouse to work as men do in the morning time."

"Ah, nonsense," the father would answer; "we can any of us dream who are too stupid to wake and too idle to work.

If it were not that he could sing I would have no patience with him."

The strange thing about Tony's song was that no one knew how he had come be it. He sang a little bit of it in the days when he looked for edelweiss seek for the little white flowers that grow on the edge of the snow on the Alps, and when he brought any back they were tied in bunches and offered for sale to the strangers. That was before he had grown so silent, before the time when the great cobweb seemed to have wrapped him round, before he wandered into a dream and shut the door on the waking world. One day he came back with his basket empty.

"But where is the edelweiss?" his mother asked.

"I did not see any," he answered, and sat down beside the smoking wood. Then he began the song he had known since he could sing at all; but this time there was something that his mother had never heard before.

"Where didst thou learn that?" she asked, but Tony would not speak.

"It is hard on thee," Gaspard's wife said, "that thy son should be a fool."

"Nay, he is no fool," the mother answered.

"But he cannot tell even where he learnt his song," the woman said.

"He learnt it in the clouds, or on the mountain side, farther up than our feet can climb--what may be there—only the like of Tony can tell," and she waited scornfully for Gaspard's wife to go; but then she sighed sadly enough.

"Surely he will someday awaken," she though, "or what will be the good of him?" But from that time Tony forgot more and more the things he was told to do, and lived among his dreams, which grew so tangled that even he could not tell the sleeping from the waking ones.

It was only in the summer that the days passed thus.

When the storms came and the snow descended, the hotels and all the chalets on the mountains were closed, and the peasant and the herdsmen and their families and their flocks went down to the valley for the winter. Tony and his parents lived with a neighbour at the entrance to the village, all of them huddled together in a wooden dwelling. The floods came, and the winds swept past, and the snow-drift piled higher and higher against the windows till it was hardly possible for any light to enter the close and smoky room. Tony used to watch his father cutting bits of wood: chip by chip he seemed to take away the walls that held little animals and men and women in prison. He never realized that his father's sharp knife and precise eye shaped the toys, or understood that it was just for the sake of the money they would bring that his mother placed them away so carefully till the dealer from Geneva came to buy them, or till it was time to put them on a tray outside the chalet door so that the strangers might see and bargain for them.

One winter there was a dark knotty morsel of wood that fascinated him. Every morning as he drank his milk his eyes wandered toward it. In the evening as he crouched shiveringly by the smouldering fire beneath the black soup-pot, he kept his eyes fixed on it and wondered what strange thing it concealed. One day his father took it up, and, turning it over and over, began to cut, till there came forth the figure of a little woman who had on her face an expression of listening and waiting. Tony's father looked at her and held her up before him when he had taken off the last bits of wood that clung to her.

"Maybe thou are expecting someone to come and bear thee company," he said, speaking to it affectionately, as though it were a child; "but I do not know of any thou canst have, unless Tony here will please thee?"

Tony shrinking back fancied that the woman's eyes turned towards him.

"She is only wood, my lad," his mother said, "and to-morrow she will be sent to the dealer's far off--there is nothing to be afraid of, she cannot move, and in things that cannot move no danger lies. All things that live and move have power to frighten, but not this bit of wood that has been shaped by thy father's knife."

But Tony crept out of the chalet and trampled the soft snow under foot, and he was afraid of the little wooden woman lying still and wide-eyed in the smoky chalet. When he went back his mother looked up and said, just as if she had divined his thoughts, "Our neighbours Louis has gone to Geneva to look for mules for the summer; he has taken all thy father's carving with him, so thou needst not be afraid of the little woman anymore."

This had happened more than year ago, and Tony had forgotten the piece of wood and what had come from it. Now his father was carving again, and making ready for the dealer who arrived once a year to buy their winter's work from the peasants; and if the dealer would not buy, the little figures would be put away in a drawer ready for the strangers.

"If I were but like one of them," Tony used to think as he saw them wrapped in soft paper, "to be always little, to be handled tenderly and put to sleep in a drawer till the summer, and then to be warmed through and through by the sun. Why should they have legs that never ache and hands that never work?"

It was a cold morning when the dealer came--a dark, silent man, black haired, with overhanging eye-brows.

"Who is this?" he asked, looking at Tony.

"He is my son," the father said; "but little enough good is he save to sing."

"Is he the boy whose song the goatherds say was learnt in the clouds?"

"It may be."

"Ah, Tony's song is known all down the valley and over the mountain too," his mother said.

"A stranger came to Geneva once and tried to sing it," the dealer said, "but he could not remember it all."

"It is no good to Tony," the father said, "he is only a fool, and will not use his hands and feet." Then the mother spoke up for her son.

"Don't judge him harshly," she said. "Surely, some are made to use their hands and some their feet, and some it may be just their hearts to feel and their lips to speak. Does he not sing a song he has fetched from the clouds? Let that travel instead of his feet and work instead of his hands."

"He is called the Wooden-head," the father went on, unheeding, "and he might well be all wooden but for his song. The rest of him is no good--"

"A song has something lived longer than the strongest hands that ever worked for bread, and travelled farther than the swiftest runner," said the mother.

"--And he would be like one of those," the father added, pointing to the little carved figures he had made.

"They were hidden in a block of wood, just as thy song is hidden in thee," his mother said, looking at Tony fondly.

"He would be better without his song," his father said. "He might dream less and work more."

The dealer considered and was silent, and when he spoke again he spoke slowly.

"Let him go to the city with me--to Geneva," he said, "and I will take the song from his lips and send it over the world."

"Tony," asked his father, "wilt thou go to Geneva? Perhaps there thou wouldst get thy wish to be far off and very little."

"Ah!" said the mother, with a heart that stood still, "but I have heard it said that a wish and its fulfillment sometimes find themselves strange company. But go if thou wilt, dear lad, there is much in the world. I would not keep thee from seeing it."

The peasants came out of their chalets and stood at their doors watching Tony as he went through the village with the dealer; but Tony did not see them. He walked as one who was dazed. The icicles hung like a fringe on the waterfall, and everywhere the sun had kissed it there rested a little golden star; but he did not look up as he passed by. He kept his eyes toward the long, straight road, and wondered if in the stems of the fir-trees beside it there dwelt strange figures like those his father had set free with his knife. The dealer pulled some wire from his pocket and fashioned it carefully as he walked on, but he said no word until the village was far behind and they could no longer hear the trickle of the unfrozen water. Then he looked up and said,

"Sing."

Mechanically, as though he were a puppet, of which the string had been pulled, Tony began to sing, and the dealer twanged the wire in his hands till it almost echoed the song. But Tony did not hear it. Over his senses had stolen a great rest; he walked as though before him he saw the land of his dreams and presently would enter its gateway.

Twang, twang, went the wire.

The fir-trees swayed a very little in the breeze; more and more as the twilight deepened, as the night came on. Tony turned his face toward them; he felt as if he knew them, he wanted to go to them, to walk among them as his friends, but something held him and he could not. The trees knew him and held out their arms: they whispered a message but he did not understand it. But he was going to understand them, to learn their language and ponder their secrets.

Twang, twang, went the wire.

The trees were wrapped in darkness at last, but Tony did not stop, he went on, on and on without stopping, into the blackness till that too was behind, and towards him slowly stole the morning light. There was a range of low mountains far in the distance. They rose higher and higher as he drew near if to greet him.

"Sing," said the dealer.

But his song was different, it seemed no longer to come from his heart but only from his lips, and as he sang he heard the notes repeated. The song was going out of him and on to the dealer's wire. He did not look toward it, he did not care; he felt nothing keenly. His legs were growing stiff and his feet were hard, yet lighter to lift than they had been. He was not tired, or warm, or cold, or glad, or sorry, but only in a dream

The fir-trees were far, far behind now. Tony and the dealer had passed other villages than the one from which they had started yesterday. They were nearer to the mountains that had looked so low at first, and before them was a blue lake reflecting the bluer sky. Beside the lake was a long road that led to the city of Geneva--the city toward which they were journeying. But there were more villages and little towns to go through first--towns with white houses on the hill-side and others low down close to the water's edge. There were carved wooden balconies to some of them, and some were built altogether of wood. Tony wondered in what strange forest the trees of which they were made had grown. He seemed to have more and more kinship with the things that belonged to Nature's firstness-- with the sky and the lake and the trees nay, even with the dead wood that had been used on human dwelling-places. But toward human beings he felt a strangeness spring up in his heart as if between him and them had begun a separation. They seemed to be made of a different texture, of different flesh and blood from himself, and they — these people— were so tall, they overshadowed him; they took long steps and carried great loads that would have crushed him. And yet they did not look bigger than his father and mother, it was only when they were beside him that he realized the difference in height. It did not surprise him, for nothing surprised him now, or stirred his pulse, or made his heart beat quicker. He went on, on.

The dealer twanged the wire, and the music of it grew more and more to resemble Tony's song. But Tony trampled in silence looking at the lake and sky, while the sun shone, and the mountains rose higher and higher. He felt as if they were his parents or had been once in a far-off time, and now they were reaching out to him trying once more to bring him back to themselves before it was forever too late. Too late for what? He did not know, he could not answer himself. His heart was growing still and slow, his lips were growing dumb.

"Sing," said the man again.

Then Tony opened his mouth, but the words of his song had gone, he could not remember them, he could not say them, only the notes came forth, but they had no meaning that could be written down in words, and each listener heard them differently. Gradually instead of singing he listened, for his song was all around and about, but it did not come from behind him, but when he tried to turn he could not. He was clasped everywhere by the wire, and in the midst of its cold tangle he walked, strange and rigid, as if in a dream. One arm hung by his side, he could not move it; one hand was in his pocket, he could not pull it out. His clothes seemed to have changed, to have grown as stiff as he, and to be separate from him no more. Only his feet moved just enough to carry him forward, and that was all.

But now the last miles of the road were behind, and the sounds of a city were before him with lines of houses standing up high and white, and many little windows like gaping mouths talking in the air or lidless eyes looking out on the people in the streets. Lower down there were windows, reaching to the ground, filled with all manner of things to please those who had money to go in and buy. Tony walked by all scarcely knowing: but he understood, for he had seen his shadow: he was in the distance towards which he had looked so often from his mountain home.

He was far off and very little.

He knew that he was bound and a prisoner, but it did not matter, he did not care. It was only part of a new life in the new world that he had entered. Suddenly with a jerk he stopped by one of the great windows; a door opened and he entered. All about him was wooden--wooden houses and people and animals-- and everywhere a sound of ticking. Tick, tick, tick. He was lifted by the dealer's hand on to a height. Before him was house, a chalet, with a flight of stairs outside leading to a balcony.

"Go up," the dealer said, and slowly stair by stair he went, his feet growing stiffer and stiffer with ever step upward. He rested on the balcony; there were two little doors leading into the house, they opened suddenly and disclosed a little room behind. In the room waiting—surely waiting for him? was the strange little woman Tony had seen his father take from the block of wood. He remembered that he used to be afraid of her. How foolish he had been; now he was afraid of nothing. He took his place beside her, he felt that they would never be apart again unless great change or sorrow came: surely it was like a marriage? He saw that the little woman was as big as he, had she grown? or had he--but he could not think or reason. He was jerked back, the wire twanged, the doors closed, and all was still. He was in the darkness waiting too, but for what or how long he did not know: all time was the same to him, he could measure it no more.

In the distance he heard other wires twanging, and presently the melody of his song came from many directions, as though the place were full of it. He could hear the people in the street; they hummed it as they passed by. Once far off he heard a band playing it. But he did not listen long, for all things grew faint as they would have grown dim too had he been in the light to se and know. For Tony's life had gone into his song; only a simple little song, just as his had been a simple little life.

Life is not only in nodding heads, and work is not only for hands that move and feet that walk; it is in many other things.

After a time there were sounds of fitting and tapping over Tony's head, a loud ticking-- tick, tick, tick unceasingly, and then a strange whirring and an iron tongue struck out clang-clang up to eleven. As the last stroke fell the little doors flew open and Tony and his companion were jerked out by the wire that bound them on to the balcony at the top to the stairs by which he had mounted, and stood together while all around and above the song was played-- the song that never would come from his lips again. Before them, separating the place in which their dwelling was from the street, was a great window letting in a flood of light, and on the outer side against the glass were pressed eager faces watching; but Tony and his companion did not know this; as the last not died away they were jerked back into the little room and all was darkness till another hour had passed, and then it all happened again. Hour after hour it was always the same, day after day, week after week, month after month, in light and dark, in heat and cold.

Two weary faces once were pressed against the window, those of a woman and a man, and as the doors opened and the two little figures came forth on the clock and stood while the song was played, the woman cried,

"It is Tony, it is Tony, it is his song; there beside him is the woman you made, and he is wooden too-- he is wooden."

"Thou art dreaming," said the man; "Tony is gone into the world, and we will go and seek him."

"No, no," the woman cried in despair, "his song has gone into the world, but Tony is there," and she pointed to the clock; "he is wooden-- he is wooden." The man looked long and silently.

"He had always a wooden head," he answered slowly; "maybe the rest of him has gone wooden too, for he did not move enough to keep quickened. But he was useless," he added, trying to comfort his wife; "didst thou not say thyself that his song would work instead of his hands, and journey instead of his feet?"

"Ah, that was well enough for those who did not love him," said the mother, "but it does not comfort me. It is Tony that I want, my son Tony who sat by the door and sang, or by the fire watching the wood smoulder." While she spoke the song, ceased, the figures were jerked into the darkness, and the doors closed; before the man and woman lay the long road and the weary miles that led back to the village and the mountains.

THE END

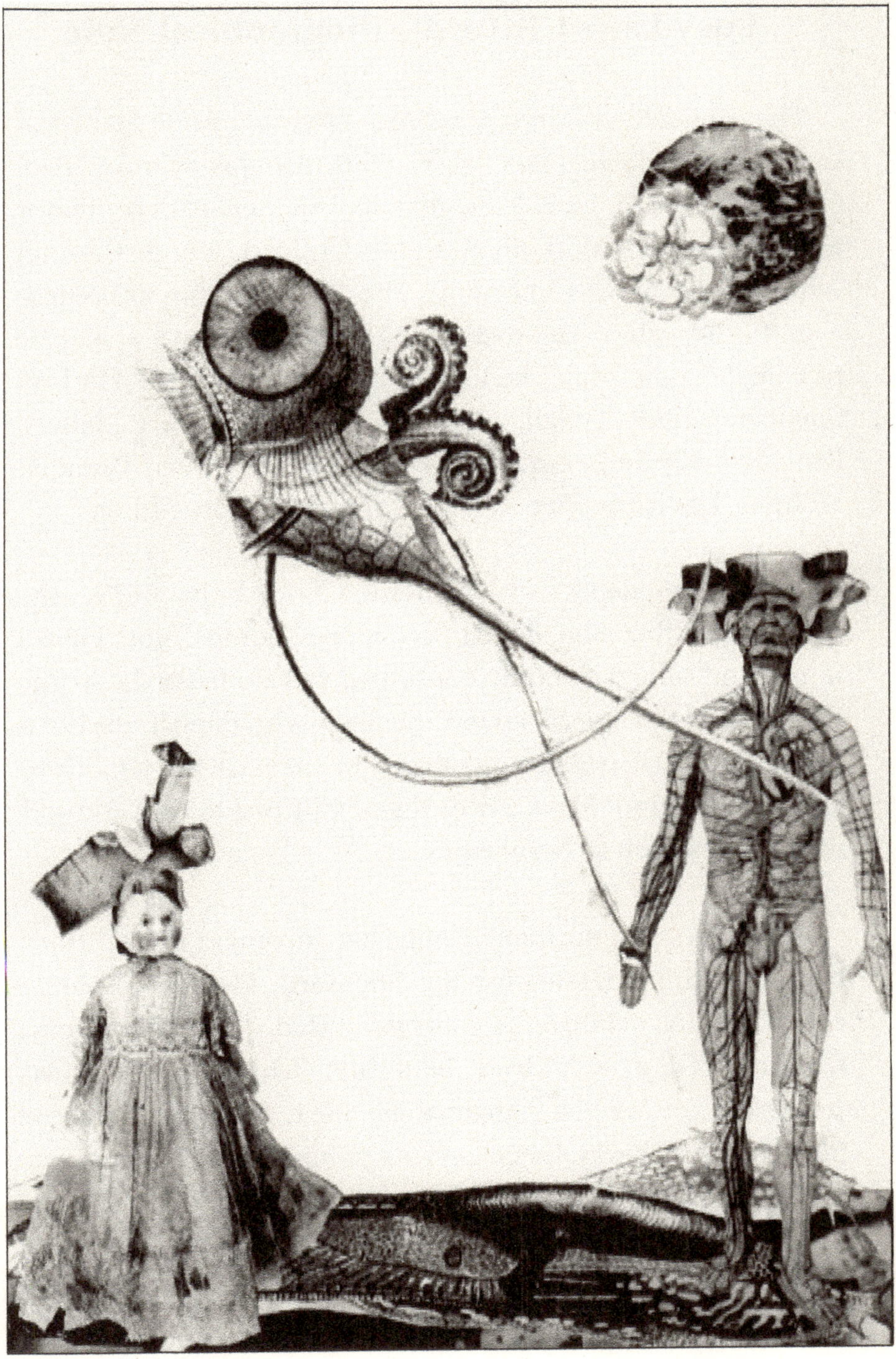

Lucy Lane Clifford – Biographical Note

The English children's writer, novelist, and dramatist Lucy Lane Clifford (Mrs. W. K. Clifford) was born in 1846. On April 7, 1875, Lucy Lane married mathematics professor and philosopher William Kingdon Clifford, whom she met while studying art in London. The Cliffords' home became a gathering place for distinguished literary and scientific persons of the day, including Charles Darwin, Herbret Spencer, John Tynall, Thomas Huxley, Henry James, Rudyard Kipling, James Russell Lowell, Oliver Wendell Holmes, Leslie Stephen, Violet Hunt, and George Eliot.

After the death of William Clifford in 1879, the friendships that she developed with George Eliot, Henry James and others not only continued but flourished. George Eliot, who was one of several persons who contributed to a small Civil List pension arranged to support Lucy Clifford and her two daughters, encouraged Clifford to find comfort in activities such as her writing.

As a means of supplementing her income, Lucy Clifford began writing reviews for the Standard. Her first book, a collection of children's stories titled Children Busy, Children Glad, Children Naughty, Children Sad, was published by Wells, Gardner in 1881. In 1882 Anyhow Stories, Moral and Otherwise was published by Macmillan.

In addition to children's fiction, Mrs. Clifford wrote novels, collections of adult stories, and later in life a number of plays. In her adult fiction, Clifford presented a variety of female characters that displayed some of the strength and independence which she exhibited in her own life. Such women appear in her novels, Aunt Anne and Mrs. Keith's Crime; her collections of stories, The Last Touches and Other Stories (1892) and Mere Stories (1896); and her play, A Woman Alone (1898).

Lucy Clifford died on April 21, 1929

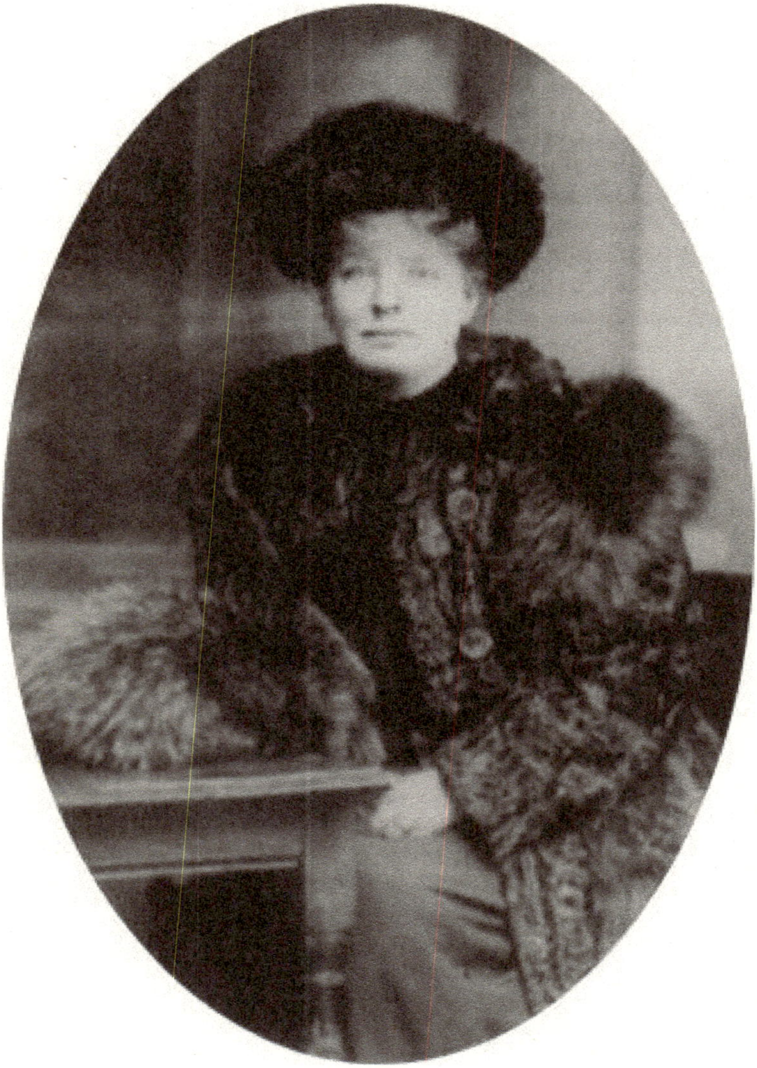

ONEIROS BOOKS are published in association with Paraphilia Magazine. www.paraphiliamagazine.com

If you enjoyed this book, you might enjoy these titles from Paraphilia Books:

THE SEVENTH SONG OF MALDOROR
D M Mitchell

A deranged serial-killer goes on a rampage of sexual atrocity across a Europe falling apart in the wake of an unspecified global crisis. But is he what he seems? A cast of implausible characters in a (to say the least) unreliable narrative push the boundaries of credibility and expression. Dreams and nightmares, desire and delirium, all melt together into a metatextual puzzle. A psycho-sexual anti-novel that owes much to its transgressive ancestors – Sade, Lautreamont, Bataille, Artaud with more than a dash of Burroughs and Lovecraft thrown into the cauldron.

Paperback: 186 pages

Language: English

ISBN-10: 1449518125

ISBN-13: 978-1449518127

(www.paraphiliamagazine.com/books.html)

THE MEMBRANOUS LOUNGE
Hank Kirton

Welcome To The Membranous Lounge! Where ugliness and beauty melt and run together, where reality is temperamental and the boundary between "normal" and grotesque is nebulous.

The Membranous Lounge is a zone of slippage, a twilight area between the layers of the world that are familiar and the terrifyingly unknown. It is a chimerical realm inhabited by the hopeless, dispossessed, and those who have simply turned away.

Imagine if Ray Bradbury and Jerri Cain Rossi had a child that they locked away from the world, with only the Marquis De Sade for reading matter, and a dietary intake of bad LSD and atrocious B Movies. The Membranous Lounge would be the spawn of that child's imagination.

With an introduction by Jim Rose

Paperback; 140 pages
Language: English
ISBN-10: 1452816301
IABN-13: 9781452816302

(www.paraphiliamagazine.com/books.html)

PARASITE (VOLUME ONE) PARASITE LOST
D M Mitchell

When David Michael K visited The Doctor's office, housed in the mysterious Building, he hadn't anticipated his life tipping into madness where reality melted and stretched and fiction merged with real life. In a satirical romp that sends up postmodernism, popular culture and satirises satire itself, our hero is chased by homicidal drug-dealing clowns, cartoon characters, pink UFOs and creatures of pure nightmare. Is this a serious book disguised as humour? or a joke at the expense of the intelligentsia? Fun stuff.

With an introduction by **Michael Roth**
Cover by **Pablo Vision**

Paperback: 274 Pages
Language: English
ISBN-10: 1453819304
ISBN-13: 978-1453819302

(www.paraphiliamagazine.com/books.html)

MESSAGES TO CENTRAL CONTROL
A D Hitchin

A shifting collage of condensed micro-novels; intense and corrosive uzi-bursts of poetic anti-narrative from some alternative cyberporn universe intersecting ours. Reading this book is like surfing the shortwave band and finding oneself listening to alien soundtracks.

"*Messages to Central Control* is a daring and challenging work, and from the outset notions of stable form, content and author are all thrown into question, and the reader is compelled to leave everything they believe in at the door, and to enter with eyes – and mind – open."

From the introduction by **Christopher Nosnibor**

With artwork by **D M Mitchell**

Paperback: 216 pages
Language: English
ISBN-10: 1453865853

(www.paraphiliamagazine.com/books.html)

A DREAM OF STONE
(and other ghost stories)
Edited by Díre McCain and D M Mitchell

A posthuman ghost anthology from the people who bring you Paraphilia Magazine.

"Their name is legion and they stalk among us. Daily tabloids are replete with pages of phone numbers where, for a fee, we can talk with nameless incubi/succubae. Alternatively, we can venture into the twilight world of the internet, and converse with 'people' who may or may not exist – the technological equivalent of planchette and Ouija board. Who knows what's really on the other end, fastening onto our insecurities, desires, and fears?"

Paperback: 330 pages
ISBN-10: 1466437944
ISBN-13: 978-1466437944

(www.paraphiliamagazine.com/books.html)

TWILIGHT FURNITURE

Posthuman pornography from the publishers of Paraphilia Magazine. Like Beckett's *How It Is* crossed with Pierre Guyotat's *Eden, Eden, Eden*.

Warning! Reading this book in one sitting might prove emotionally disturbing.

Paperback: 174 pages

Language: English

ISBN-10: 1453709835

(www.paraphiliamagazine.com/books.html)

And please check out the free online magazine at:
www.paraphiliamagazine.com/magazine.html

Printed in January 2023
by Rotomail Italia S.p.A., Vignate (MI) - Italy